A SISTER'S
SECRET

RUDY ANN PUTTON

A Sister's Secret
Copyright © 2023 Written by Rudy Ann Putton

Tellwell Talent
www.tellwell.ca

ISBN
978-0-2288-8837-6 (Paperback)
978-0-2288-8838-3 (eBook)

This book is dedicated to my husband,
Silvano
for always being my rock.

CHAPTER 1

SKYLAR WAS STARTING TO COME around. She was having a tough time focusing. Her eyelids were heavy, her head was foggy, and it felt as heavy as a bowling ball. She could barely hold it up. "What's happened to me?" she asked herself. She had no idea where she was, how she got to this place or how long she'd been here. The room smelled like death. Like a piece of rotting meat. It was awful. The mattress she was lying on smelled like urine. She managed to roll over and tried to get up on her hands and knees but was too weak and fell down on the mattress. So close to the edge, her hand hit the floor. The floor was cold. The room had no windows. The only light that came in was from the bottom of a door, at the top of the stairs. Her wrists and ankles were sore from tugging on the bindings that restrained her. The way she felt, she must have been drugged? She couldn't remember anything. She knew she was going to die if she didn't find a way out. She heard footsteps coming from the top floor and soon afterwards, the door opened. A bright light was turned on, blinding her. She rolled over and managed to sit up, putting her arms up in front of her eyes, trying to keep them open so she could see who it was, but her eyes felt like they were on fire. She had to close them. Who was coming down the stairs? She could hear footsteps coming closer.

"Who are you? Where am I? Answer me. Why are you doing this? Why?"

Suddenly, she was slapped across the face. Skylar's left cheek was on fire, and she cried out. Skylar fell over on her side. "*You know what you did bitch.*" The male voice said.

Skylar somewhat regained her composure and sat up slowly. With her long hair tousled and all over of her face, she began yelling at the stranger, who she still couldn't see. She just couldn't focus.

"Tell me what I did, because I have no fucking clue what you're talking about."

His voice sounded familiar, Skylar thought, but her brain couldn't make the connection for her to remember. She was trying really hard to remember but she was too weak, anxious, and scared. She was shaking and continued to cry. Her brain was still foggy, and she couldn't put her thoughts together. She stuttered when she spoke.

He turned away from Skylar and she could barely make out an image of him now. The last thing she remembered was having great sex with Morgan. This can't be Morgan. She remembers him leaving her apartment or maybe he didn't. She just couldn't remember.

"*You're a slut. You know what you did.*" He moved closer to her. Almost face to face and now she could see him.

Skylar recognized him. "This can't be. Not you." She was completely stunned and speechless. Her eyes now as big as globes. She couldn't believe it, "its you, but why? Why are you doing this to me?" He loved seeing the fear in her eyes. It brought him such immense pleasure.

"*You know what you did and now you will pay for it.*" He threatened.

"You're going to rape me? Please no! Don't do this. Please don't." Skylar pleaded.

"*Rape you. Never. I don't want you after you've had him. You're nothing but a slut.*" The male voice said, with a grin on his face.

Skylar had a look of confusion on her face. "Had who? Who are you talking about? What are you talking about?" Skylar had no clue what he was talking about. She was yelling at him, crying, she was so frustrated. Her voice was cracking. "You're a crazy bastard. Let me out of this hell hole, she demanded."

"*Shut up you bitch.*" He said. "Please let me go. I'll do whatever you want. Please." Skylar was begging him now.

Skylar didn't see the knife. He smiled at her as he plunged the knife into her body, just below her rib cage. He looked at her face, loving her expression of total confusion and surprise. Her mouth open and eyes wide. She just stared at him as he took the knife out and plunged it into her once again. He stared right back at her smiling, as he found his release.

As Skylar lay dying, with her voice barely a whisper, she was calling out for Jade and then everything went dark.

CHAPTER 2

J<small>ADE HADN'T HEARD FROM HER</small> younger sister Skylar in almost two weeks, which was unlike her. They spoke on the phone at least twice a week. Jade had called several times during the past week and left a few messages but didn't hear back from her sister. She decided to drive from her home in Sault Ste. Marie to Sudbury. She had vacation time and Northern, Ontario is beautiful in June, she thought.

Jade decided, as a last resort, to call her sister's place of employment to speak to her, but she was told Skylar was off for a few days.

"Skylar better have a good reason for not calling me back. She knows I'm going to worry." She said to herself.

The drive took three and a half hours. When she arrived at her sister's apartment at Glen Birch, she noticed the door looked shut, but was slightly ajar. This wasn't in her sister's character. Skylar was adamant about locking the door even when she was home. She would never leave it open or unlocked. She slowly pushed the door open and took a few steps in and called for Skylar. She heard nothing. She looked around, standing close to the door, and noticed nothing was out of place. Jade took a few more steps in causing the apartment door to shut but not close. Skylar's purse and cell phone were on the kitchen counter. Jade knew her sister would never go anywhere without her purse, and certainly wouldn't forget her cell phone. She was worried before but now she was scared. She knew her sister was in trouble. Jade immediately called 911.

Detective Mark Ross was sitting at this desk. It was mid afternoon, and he had a ton of paperwork he needed to complete before his shift was over. He thought the noise in this squad room is unbelievable today. Phones ringing non-stop, and people talking over each other were driving him nuts or maybe it just seemed noisy because the headache that was coming on was going to split his head in two. Officer Tilley asked him if he would take a call from central intake about a missing person. Picking up the phone, he quickly identified himself "Detective Ross."

Jade reiterated her story about her sister, Skylar. Jade made it clear to Detective Ross that she knows something is wrong. Detective Ross attempted to calm this woman, as she was hysterical. He was having trouble understanding her as she was very emotional, crying, and just kept talking. More like rambling. He couldn't get a word in edgewise. He could tell she was scared out of her mind.

"Ms. Rose, you need to calm down and answer some questions. May I have the address please." There was no point in asking this woman questions on the phone. He knew he wasn't going to get anywhere with her unless he met with her. She was too anxious. Jade rambled off the address to her sister's apartment.

Detectives Ross and Shapiro had been partners for the last seven years. They were the best of friends, who didn't always see eye to eye but there was a mutual respect. They worked missing persons and homicide. Ross was the younger of the two at thirty-eight years of age. He was tall, dark, and handsome. The ladies liked him; Shapiro would say. He was single. Shapiro was tall, and handsome for an older gentleman of fifty-two years. He was graying around the temples and married. Ross did the leg work and Shapiro did more of the paperwork and research.

Detective Ross knocked on the apartment door and Jade quickly answered. "Ms. Rose, I'm Detective Ross and this is my partner, Detective Shapiro." Both showed their credentials.

"Please come in," Jade said.

They walked into a one-bedroom apartment that was nicely decorated with black, white, and gray colors. Plants weren't wilted and were cared for. Ross thought, she couldn't have been gone for too long. The place was clean, no odors and the garbage can was nearly empty. It seemed like everything was in its proper place. The bed wasn't made. There certainly weren't any signs that a struggle had occurred. Jade and both detectives sat at the kitchen table.

Detective Ross started by asking Jade if she had moved anything or touched anything. She hadn't. She had only closed the door which she found open and checked the bedroom window latch, which was secure, as the apartment was on the ground level.

"Ms. Rose, what is your full name and address."

"Jade Ann Rose. 735 Main Street, unit two, Sault Ste. Marie."

"You don't live here?" Detective Ross asked curiously.

"No, I drove here because I haven't been able to reach my sister for the last two weeks. I arrived about fifteen minutes before I called you."

"Why do you believe your sister is missing or something has happened to her?"

"We speak on the phone at least twice a week and I can't get a hold of her. I've left numerous messages, but she hasn't responded. This is not like her. She never leaves the door open or unlocked and it was ajar when

I got here. Her purse and cell phone are here, but she isn't. Her car isn't here either. Something is not right. Something has happened to Skylar. Please believe me. I'm not being over dramatic. I know my sister. All we have is each other. Our parents died in a car accident seven years ago."

Detective Shapiro asked, "when was the last time you spoke to your sister? Did she seem like she was in any distress or was having any problems?"

Jade thought about the last conversation she had with her sister ten days ago. She remembered her sister was tired from all the overtime she was doing at Holy Angels Hospital, but she wasn't distressed. "I spoke to her about ten days ago and there was nothing out of the ordinary. Skylar expressed she was tired. She was working a lot of overtime and was planning to enroll in a new online course, to help further her career."

"What does she do for a living," Detective Ross asked.

"She's a Registered Nurse. She works in the emergency department, at Holy Angels."

"Does she have a significant other?"

Jade smiled stating "no, according to Skylar, she is to busy and has no time for a relationship."

"Does she have any enemies? Anyone she has been arguing with or anything of that nature?"

Jade thought about their conversations and couldn't recall anything like that. "No, nothing I can recall or know about. People like Skylar. She gets along with everybody."

"Has she been known to use drugs or have one-night stands?" When Detective Shapiro asked the question, he already knew the answer. Looking at the missing woman's apartment, she was neat and organized. Very prim and proper. She didn't strike him as the type.

Jade was annoyed by the question." My sister is not, nor was she ever a drug user. She has never used drugs. She didn't' smoke either. She enjoyed sex with no strings attached from time to time. However, she wouldn't have sex with someone she just met or didn't know."

Detective Ross asked Jade if she knew any of the men her sister was having occasional sex with. Jade didn't know any of them.

"Ms. Rose, we need a recent picture of your sister." Jade complied with the request. She took a picture out of her wallet and gave it to Ross.

Jade explained "this is the last photo of us together. It was taken six months ago at a friend's birthday party. She looks the same today. Skylar is twenty-eight years old"

Ross thought, Skylar is a beautiful woman. A brunette with long brown hair and big brown eyes. Her smile is infectious. He could tell she was younger than Jade and by the way she was hugging her sister, there was a close bond. Beauty must run in the family. As soon as he laid eyes on Jade, when she opened the door, he did a double take. She was gorgeous. A brunette with wavy hair down to her waist, beautiful big baby blue eyes a man could get lost in and skin that was like porcelain. She was tall and had an incredible figure, with beautiful full lips, ample breasts, long legs and curvy, but narrow hips. He also noticed that she wasn't wearing a wedding band or engagement ring. Detective Ross took the picture. He also reminded Jade to call if she hears from Skylar or has any further information. Ross gave her his card.

"Are you going back to the Sault or staying in town Ms. Rose?"

"I'm going to stay in town until I know what is going on with my sister. I have vacation time from work."

Ross asked, "what do you do for a living Ms. Rose?"

"Please call me Jade. I'm a chef."

Ross explained, "we'll be conducting door to door inquiries in the apartment complex. Maybe someone saw something."

Detective Shapiro suggested she take a hotel room while in town, rather than staying at her sister's place. "We don't exactly know what happened here, at your sister's place. It would be safer for you to stay elsewhere."

The detectives also informed Jade that her sister's picture may be given to the local news media to assist in locating her, if needed. Jade knew this was something that had to be done, but it would mean her sister was really missing and could be hurt, or worse. She began to cry.

"Do what you need to do. Please find my sister."

"We'll be in touch Ms. Rose." Ross reassured her, and he and Shapiro left.

Jade composed herself and called the Bella Cucina Restaurant where she was employed in Sault Ste. Marie. She explained there was a family emergency and needed some time off. Later she would need to check into a hotel and get herself settled. She needed her sister found. She needed to know Skylar was safe.

CHAPTER 3

DETECTIVE ROSS WAS AT HIS desk bright and early the next morning. He had already had a pot of coffee. Didn't seem to help. He got little sleep and still had the same headache, he had from the day before. It was lingering. He opened the top drawer of his desk and popped two aspirins. His eight-hour shift the day before, turned into a twelve-hour day by the time he and Shapiro spoke to the other tenants of the apartment complex where Skylar Rose lived. He also finished the paperwork that was on his desk.

One of the tenants, Ms. Tina Lipton, who was middle aged and lived across from the victim told him "She is a friendly but quiet girl, you wouldn't know she lived there, but she does have male companions that visit. I've seen a tall man visit in the evening. Maybe twice a week, but I don't know his name. At times, I've seen her leaving her apartment late at night, when most people are going to bed. I don't think she was working the graveyard shift because she wasn't wearing her nursing uniform."

Ross thought, this woman is one of those nosy neighbours that knows everything about the people living in her complex. For him, she was a god send. Ross wondered who the guy was and where she was going late at night.

Officer Tilley came over to Ross' desk, "I just received a call from an anonymous caller! The caller explained there is a body in the park behind Holy Angels Hospital."

"Did the caller say anything else? Was the person a male or female?" Detective Ross asked.

"He didn't say anything else. I wanted to transfer the call over to you, but the guy said what he said and just hung up," Officer Tilley explained.

Ross grabbed his jacket hanging on the back of his chair and cell phone from the top of his desk, and took off, walking to his car. He called his partner and drove to Gage Park. By the time he got there, the police had secured the area. CSI technicians started collecting evidence near the body as well as taking multiple photos. A standard police drape had been placed over the body. The media started arriving but was kept at bay, however that didn't stop them from yelling out questions. The body was to far away for bystanders and news reporters to see it. It was lying under some shrubbery, almost hidden. As Ross got closer, he noticed Officer Frasier was securing the area.

"What do we have Frasier?"

"Dead female sir. Looks like she's been stabbed."

Ross lifted the drape just enough to observe. The body was a Caucasian female between the ages of twenty-five and thirty-five. She looked dishevelled. She had a tee shirt and underwear on. Her hair was matted, and the body smelled like urine. Ross could see stab wounds and bruising to the face. He thought, this Jane Doe looks a lot like Skylar Rose.

Detective Shapiro found his partner and asked, "what do we have Mark?"

Ross shared his thoughts and observations with him and told him "We're waiting for the coroner before we touch or move the body."

Dr. Eric Lind had a reputation for being one of the best in his field. He was a tall, heavy-set man, with thick glasses, and a no-nonsense attitude. Dr. Lind walked over to the body and crouched down to examine the deceased.

Mark thought, for being such a big man, he had no trouble crouching down. Dr. Lind completed a brief preliminary examination of the body and determined that unofficially, until an autopsy was completed, the cause of death or C.O.D. was possibly due to exsanguination. He noted two large stab wounds to the upper right side of the victims torso. He ordered the body be transported back to the morgue for autopsy.

The autopsy was a lengthy one taking approximately four hours. As Medical Examiner he concluded, the female on his table was killed by two fatal stab wounds to just below the right rib cage, puncturing the right lung and slicing the hepatic vein. There was no damage to the inferior vena cava. The stab wounds also caused spillage of her intestines. Ross and Shapiro entered the morgue about five hours after the body was transported to the morgue. The coroner was just signing the death certificate. Dr. Lind stepped out of the lab. He met them both in the hallway.

"I am ruling this death a homicide gentlemen," he said.

Ross asked, "how long has she been dead?"

Dr. Lind estimated approximately sixteen hours, according to body temperature and the condition of the body. "Our victim was not sexually assaulted. Further, I didn't find any semen in the vaginal, oral, or anal cavity. There was bruising to the left side of her face, suggesting physical assault. Her wrists were severely bruised. She had been bound with twine. We scraped under her fingernails. The puncture wounds were measured, and the knife used was an eight-inch carving knife. There was nothing special about it. When toxicology and DNA results come in, I'll call you. Perhaps, there was DNA on the rope bindings or victim's clothing. Also, there was a faint smell of urine on the body. If anything, else is found, I will let you know. This all takes time." Dr. Lind reminded them. Fingerprints taken by Dr. Lind's assistant Kyle, belonged to Skylar Lee Rose. A twenty-eight-year-old female that had no criminal history. Her fingerprints were in the data base.

"She was a registered nurse. All hospital employees must have a criminal record check prior to being hired. That's why her fingerprints were in the system." Ross explained.

Dr. Lind continued, "Our victim was a very health young lady. Her organs were removed and weighed and there was nothing remarkable about them. Lungs were healthy. She certainly didn't smoke. Detectives this was a vicious attack. Whoever, this killer is, he wanted to inflict pain. If he had stabbed her once, she would have bled out causing her death, but twice…. he wanted to ensure her death and a painful one at that. This person has killed before."

Shapiro left to have the victim's apartment sealed off and called in for a CSI team to gather any evidence they could find and take photos. He was also going to put out a "be on the look out" or B.O.L.O on the victim's car, a burgundy Chevy Malibu, according to her sister. Shapiro needed to have financial records subpoenaed, along with the victim's computer and cell phone.

Detective Ross knew he would have to inform the next of kin. He would have to tell Jade her sister was dead. Ross told Shapiro he'd meet him at the victim's apartment later. He needed to tell Jade before she heard it on the news. Earlier, Jade had informed him of where she would be staying.

Jade had checked into the Holiday Inn on Pimm Street. She was speaking on the phone with Skylar's closest friend and co-worker, Kim Marshall. Jade explained, she came to town to see her sister and can't seem to find her.

"Skylar was always tired. She's took last week off. She asked for it off saying she wanted to get away, but she didn't tell me where she was going." Kim said.

Jade couldn't hide the shock in her voice. "She wanted to get away and go where? She never told me anything about wanting to take time off of work."

"I don't know that, but I do know she's been spending quality time with Morgan Sinclair, if you catch my drift. He's a new medical intern at the hospital. I don't know much about him but he's gorgeous."

While on the phone, Jade heard a knock on the door. She saw who it was through the peep hole and opened the door. "Kim, I need to go. I'll call you later." Detective Ross was standing there and by the look on his face, Jade knew it wasn't good news.

"Ms. Rose, may I come in?"

"Do you have any news about my sister, Detective Ross?" From the look on his face, Jade could tell the news wasn't good.

"I'm sorry to have to tell you, your sister's body was discovered this morning in the park, behind the hospital."

Jade began sobbing, "No she can't be gone. You've made a mistake. She's not gone. How?"

Ross hesitated for a moment, looking at her, "Skylar was stabbed, I'm sorry Jade."

He wanted to hold her right now and comfort her. He knew this would be unprofessional, so he backed away before he did something stupid. "Is there anyone I can call for you?"

She continued to sob. Eventually she calmed, but the tears continued to flow. "I will be fine, thank you." She knew she wouldn't be fine, and she didn't want to be alone, but she didn't want to ask Detective Ross to stay with her.

It was almost supper time and Ross knew this day wasn't going to end any time soon. He asked Jade if she needed anything. Jade needed to see her sister.

"I want to see my sister." Jade said. Detective Ross needed her to make an identification of the deceased. Ross called the morgue and asked to speak to the coroner.

Dr. Lind was asked "if the body could be prepared for viewing by the next of kin and prove of identity." Dr. Lind granted the request at this time.

Ross escorted Jade to the morgue. He introduced Jade to Dr. Lind. Dr. Lind expressed his condolences for her loss and asked her to let him know when she was ready to view her sister. He would escort her in.

"I'm ready to see my sister." Dr. Lind had the cooler open already, he pulled down the drape from the victim's face down to the shoulders, and Jade nearly fainted. Ross caught her before she hit the floor. She began sobbing, holding on to Ross. He had her in his arms this time and wasn't letting go.

"My little sister. Who would do this? Why? Why? "Ross was going to find out. Jade composed herself. Dr. Lind replaced the drape and escorted both Jade and Ross to his office. She stopped holding on to Ross and stepped out of his arms.

"My sister always wanted to be cremated. She didn't want anything big. That wasn't her. She always said she didn't want people coming to see her in a casket. She wanted people to remember her the way she was in life. I will have her cremated, as she wished and later have a celebration of her life."

"Which funeral home do you wish to have her sent to when she can be released," Dr. Lind asked.

"I'm not sure, I'm not from here. I don't know." Jade couldn't think. She just wanted to cry.

Ross interjected, "she'll get back to you tomorrow, Doc." Dr. Lind just nodded.

Ross drove Jade back to her hotel, walked her to her room and asked if there was anything else, he could do for her. Jade hadn't said anything since they left the morgue. Ross knew she was drained.

"No but thank you for all your help, detective. Please keep me updated about my sister's case. I'm going to stay here for a while. I need to get my sister's affairs in order as well, but first I need to get myself together."

Ross told her he would call her tomorrow. They both said goodnight. Jade got into bed fully clothed and cried herself to sleep.

It was almost seven p. m. by the time Ross left the hotel. He called Shapiro, while heading back to the station, and explained why he couldn't meet him at the victim's apartment. Shapiro figured as much.

"Did the apartment give us anything? Ross could hear the excitement in Shapiro's voice.

"The apartment was a wealth of information! In a locked closet, we found an appointment book with appointments scheduled late at night and meeting places, beautiful female lingerie that didn't leave much to the imagination, Gucci dresses, Prada shoes, and Louis Vuitton purses that were worth a lot of money, various blonde wigs, and kinky toys. Ten thousand dollars in cash, was also found in a locked drawer."

"What the hell was this girl into?" Ross asked.

"I don't know, but whatever it was, I'm thinking, it got her killed. I got a subpoena to look into her finances. I also have techs going through her cell phone records and personal computer."

Shapiro said what Ross was thinking "we need to look into the scheduled appointments and meeting places. Who was she meeting and what was she doing there?"

Ross was blunt, "a beautiful girl, out late at night in beautiful clothes with tiny undergarments, meeting at scheduled locations, in disguise and having a lot of liquid cash. This doesn't sound good at all. It sounds like Skylar Rose wasn't as innocent as she wanted people to believe she was."

CHAPTER 4

JADE WOKE UP AND COULDN'T move for the first while. She was numb. She hadn't slept well and tossed and turned all night. Thoughts of Skylar ran through her mind. Thoughts of happier times. When they were kids at the beach, waking up Christmas morning so excited to open their gifts, and when they each graduated from college. And now, her little sister was dead.

"Who would kill her and why?" This didn't make any sense. Jade knew it would be a mistake, but she turned on the television anyway. Her sister's murder was all over the news.

Northern Ontario, Channel 10 news anchor Kelly Belmar reporting "Police are investigating the discovery of a female body found dead in Gage Park. Officers were called to the park early yesterday morning. A police spokesperson confirmed the victim was Skylar Rose, a twenty-eight-year-old registered nurse. Police are not commenting on how she died." The local news media didn't have all the pieces of the puzzle, Jade thought.

As much as Jade wanted to crawl back into bed and forget about the world, she needed to get herself together. She needed to look after her sister's personal affairs and clean out her apartment. She needed to call Dr. Lind. He was going to assist her with arrangements to have her sister cremated. Jade was also going to speak with Kim Marshall. If anyone knew anything about the possible circumstances leading to Skylar's death it would be Kim, Skylar's best friend.

It was ten in the morning. Ross and Shapiro had been working on a game plan for the day and discussing what they had so far. They had been at the station for three hours already. They knew the victim was killed elsewhere. The park was a secondary location. There was a lack of blood where the body was discovered. In fact, there wasn't much there at all. No personal items, no footprints, no cameras in the vicinity. Nothing. The killer knew the body wouldn't be located until he called. Gage Park was more of a memorial park with two benches and a memorial plaque in the centre. It was too small to play ball or throw a frisbee. It was more of a walk-through park. The killer knew it wouldn't be populated with people that could find the body, until he called it in.

"He was obviously familiar with the area. He knew exactly what he was doing." Ross explained.

Shapiro was going to look into the victim's financial records and the appointments in the victim's appointment book. There were three appointments in the last month at the prestigious Windsor Park Hotel. All the appointments were scheduled between ten and ten-thirty p.m. Shapiro had a feeling the financial records were going to prove invaluable, considering all the money that was found in her apartment.

"I'm going to speak to the victim's supervisor. She might have confided in someone at work." Ross wanted to know who this "tall" man was that Ms. Lipton spoke of. Perhaps, the victim had worked with this person. He also told Shapiro he was going to check on Jade. "Any news on the car?"

"Nothing yet." Shapiro said.

As he was driving to the hospital, Ross thought about Jade. She had lost her parents seven years ago and now her sister was gone. She must feel so alone. He felt for her. He needed to be careful with this woman. He was attracted to her.

Dr. Lind was such a kind man, Jade thought. On the phone, he explained, "I will have your sister looked after by Blue Meadow Funeral Home and Crematorium. Gil Barnes, the owner, is a good friend of mine who is very professional and understanding. You will be in good hands and well looked after. I will give him your contact information and he will contact you. Your sister's body will be released in the next day or so. Gil will want to speak to you personally about what you would like." Jade was so grateful for the help. She felt so vulnerable.

"Thank you so much Dr. Lind for your help."

"You're welcome, Ms. Rose and again I am very sorry for your loss."

By the time Jade finished showering, it was close to noon. She checked her cell phone for messages. The owner of the restaurant called to give his condolences. Apparently, Paolo Longo recognized Skylar's name from the news.

"I remember when she came to the restaurant to surprise you, the last time she came to town. I can't believe this happened to your sister Jade. My wife and I are thinking of you and are so sorry for your loss, my dear. You take off as much time as you need. Your job will be here." Jade would eventually call Mr. Longo. He and his wife were always kind to her.

Kim Marshall also left a message. Jade could barely understand what she was saying because she was sobbing while trying to talk. "Jade, I am so sorry about Skylar. I'm not going to work today; I am completely heart broken. I lost my best friend. This can't be real. Please call me. I really want to talk to you. I'm worried about you." Kim was distraught. Jade assumed Kim must have seen the news. She called Kim and told her she would be over in about an hour. Jade needed to stay busy.

"Kim has to know something. Skylar and Kim always confided in each other." Jade said out loud.

Jade was hoping that Detective Ross would have called. He said that he would call. She felt so good in his arms yesterday when he was holding her. She didn't want to break free from him, but she needed to get herself together. She was a mess.

Ross had just finished questioning Amanda Lasalle, who was the nursing manager for the emergency department. She was a short, stout, middle aged women who played by the rules. She wore her glasses at the end of her nose. She had mostly good things to say about the victim.

Looking around, Ross noticed co-workers were emotional over the death of their colleague. It was evident, Skylar was well liked.

"Ms. Lasalle when was the last time you saw the victim?

"That would have been close to two weeks ago. She asked for last week off'"

"Did she seem more preoccupied, stressed, or different lately? How was her work performance?" Ross asked.

"Her work was meticulous. I would expect nothing less. She would never cut corners. She was an asset to this department. As far as being "different," the only thing I can think of is, she was calling in sick more often than usual."

"Do you know why?"

"No, she didn't look sick to me. I was going to speak to her about it because we are always working short. Before she would always pick up overtime shifts. I don't know what had changed."

"Do you know if she was keeping company with anyone?"

"She and Morgan Sinclair, a new intern, were sleeping together. I know they were. It wasn't serious. No strings attached or friends with benefits. I think that's what the young people call it."

"Is Sinclair here today?"

"No, he just finished a rotation of three-night shifts. He has the next two days off."

Ross was curious, "by any chance is Sinclair a tall man?"

"Yes, he's, about 6'3."

Ross thought, Sinclair is probably the "tall man" Ms. Lipton was talking about.

"Ms. Lasalle did Ms. Rose have a close friend at work. Someone she would confide in?"

"Kim Marshall was her best friend. She called in today, taking a personal day. When she called, she was sobbing, I could barely make out what she was saying. She wasn't fit to work."

"I'll need her address and Mr. Sinclair's as well."

"Of course. Detective Ross, something had changed with Skylar. She wasn't herself. We work twelve hours shifts and lately besides calling in sick more often, Skylar would trade off her night shifts for day shifts. She came in tired for the day shifts, all the time. I think that's why she was calling in sick more often. It seemed like she was burning the candle at both ends."

"Would you know if she had another job, Mrs. Lasalle?"

"No, I have no idea. I don't believe so. Although, she was typically so energetic and eager."

"Thank you for your assistance, Mrs. Lasalle," Ross said and left with the information he asked for.

As Ross was driving to Kim Marshall's place, he checked in with Shapiro. Shapiro had spoken with the General Manager, Mr. Seymour Hopkins, at the Windsor Park Hotel. The manager didn't recognize the victim from her photo.

"I asked him for security footage for the dates and times in question, according to the victim's appointment book." Shapiro said, "its going to take time. How bout you? You got anything?"

"The victim was sleeping with an intern at the hospital by the name of Morgan Sinclair. She was also calling in sick more often than usual. Right now, I am on my way to speak to the victim's best friend and co-worker, Kim Marshall."

Shapiro asked, "you got an address on Sinclair? I can go speak to him while the hotel is gathering the security footage." Ross rhymed off Sinclair's address.

Ross arrived at Kim Marshall's home, in Minnow Lake. It was a well-kept brick bungalow with lots of curb appeal. He rang the doorbell and waited for someone to answer the door. The woman that answered the door had been crying. Her brown eyes were blood shot, making them appear hazel. She had dark circles around her eyes, as well. Her curly hair was flat on one side, and she looked messy. She was still in her pyjamas and robe. Ms. Marshall was a petite woman that looked fragile at this moment.

"Ms. Marshall, I'm Detective Ross with Sudbury Police Services. Ross presented his badge. I'm investigating the murder of Skylar Rose. I need to ask you some questions. May I come in please?"

She began crying again. "Of course, please come in."

As Ross was walking into the living room, he saw Jade sitting on a brown leather sofa. The living room was decorated in earth tones. They made eye contact, and he must have surprised her.

"Detective Ross what are you doing here? Is this about Skylar?"

"Hello Ms. Rose."

"Please call me Jade."

"I'm here to speak to Ms. Marshall."

He looked at Kim while speaking to Jade, "its my understanding that Ms. Marshall and your sister were best friends.

"May I speak to you in private Ms. Marshall?"

Jade got up and excused herself. She was going to step outside. "I need to make a phone call," she said. She needed to call her boss, Mr. Longo.

Detective Ross could see that Jade was trying to keep it together. She looked tired and broken.

Kim looked at Detective Ross, "please sit down." Ross sat down in the matching brown leather chair to the sofa.

Once Jade was outside, Ross began his questioning. "How long had you known the victim and when did you see her last?"

"Skylar and I met at the university here in town. She was from the Sault and came here to study nursing. We spent four years in school studying, graduated, passed our provincial exams, and then got hired in the emergency department together. We had known each other for just over ten years. The last time I saw her was about a week or so, at work. We were working a twelve-hour day shift. She told me she was taking a week off, which was last week. I assumed she needed some rest from working so much. I worked all week so; I really don't know what she did during her week off. I didn't call her. Skylar called and left a message about a week ago, asking for shift exchanges for two day shifts next month."

"She left you a message?" Ross repeated.

"Yes, she did."

"Do you still have the message?"

"No, I erased it. Why?" Kim asked.

"I wanted to know which dates in question she was asking about and to hear her voice. Sometimes a person's voice can reveal how they are feeling. She could have felt tired, anxious, pressured, or scared."

Kim remembered the dates and wrote them down for Ross. He noticed the dates were for the fifteenth and sixteenth of the following month.

"So, Skylar wanted to switch for day shifts on these dates, Ross asked?"

"That's correct."

Ross was curious, "did you call her back."

"I did the next day but there was no answer, so I left her a message to call me when she had a chance."

"Had she been preoccupied or seemed different to you in any way?"

"No, I didn't notice anything different, Detective Ross, except that she was more tired, but that was pretty normal for Skylar lately."

"Had she been calling in sick more often?"

"Not that I can recall. Is there anything else? I don't want to leave Jade alone for too long."

Ross thought Ms. Marshall was evasive with her answers and she lied twice. Shapiro had subpoenaed the victim's cell phone records, including messages and texts. There weren't any messages on Skylar's cell phone from anyone when Shapiro checked it. No blinking lights or vibrations when picked up, indicating there was a message or text. Ross was going to speak to Shapiro about this. How could Kim not know that her best friend was calling in sick more often than usual, when they worked in the same department. Ross thought, she was hiding something.

"That's all for now, thanks. I have your information if I require any further assistance. Please give me a moment with Ms. Rose."

Kim just nodded, indicating she understood.

Jade was sitting outside on a lawn chair. She had just gotten off the phone with Mr. Barnes, the owner of the crematorium. All the arrangements had been made. All Jade had to do was pick out an urn for her sister's ashes.

She heard the door open and saw Detective Ross walking towards her.

"How are you doing today?" Ross asked.

"I didn't want to come out of my hotel room, but I needed to get things done, Jade said. Kim called wanting me to come over. I really didn't want to, but I thought she might have information that could help find my sister's killer."

"Did she, Ross asked?"

"Not really, all she said is that Skylar was keeping company with a new intern. A "no strings attached kind of relationship." She told me that yesterday, just before you knocked on my hotel room door."

"I know about your sister's relationship with Morgan." Ross confirmed.

Ross was curious, "how did you get here? Your car isn't out front'"

"I took a cab. I didn't want to drive. I don't know my way around Sudbury"

Ross was heading back to the station to connect with Shapiro. "Would you like a lift back to the hotel?"

"That would be wonderful, thank you."

Jade said goodbye to Kim, gave her a hug and left with Ross.

As they were driving back to the hotel, Ross made a point of telling Jade, he didn't want her investigating her sister's murder.

"You don't know who you might be talking to. Its dangerous. It could be the killer. If you have any information, let me or Detective Shapiro know, and we will look into it."

"Detective Ross its almost dinner time, have you eaten?" Jade asked.

"Your changing the subject Ms. Rose. Did you understand what I said?

"Crystal clear, now are you going to answer my question?"

"I've had a sandwich and too much coffee today. That's about it"

"Would you like to have dinner with me? I don't want to eat alone. I know that sounds …"

"Sure, we can get a bite," Ross quickly answered. He wasn't going to give up this opportunity to spend some time alone with her. He let Shapiro know he would be back at the station in about an hour.

CHAPTER 5

IT WAS FIVE P.M. BY the time they had finished dinner. They had dinner at the hotel. She was interesting. She inquired about the investigation and asked if we had made any headway. Ross explained, "we have some leads that we are following up on."

"What kind of leads?"

"Nothing I can talk about right now. Jade did you ask me to dinner to get information about the progression of the case? We just started investigating your sister's murder. I'm sorry but I don't have anything for you right now and even if I did, I can't talk to you about an ongoing investigation."

"I'm sorry Detective Ross, I'm just so angry. I just don't understand how this happened or why? My sister never walked on the dark side. She wasn't an angel, but she didn't deserve this. I want answers." Ross felt for her. For the remainder of the time, they talked about anything but the murder.

It was close to five forty-five p.m. by the time Ross got back to the station. Shapiro was on the phone with his wife. Ross was thinking of Jade and their conversation at dinner. She was five years older than her sister. A smart woman, who wasn't afraid to say exactly what was on her mind. She had never been married, nor was she attached. As a Chef, she specialized in Italian cuisine and pastries. She completed her studies at Le Cordon Bleu Culinary Arts Institute in Ottawa, Ontario.

"I don't have a life, I spend long hours at the restaurant," she mentioned. She explained she was going to talk to Skylar about moving to Sudbury, so the sisters could be closer to each other.

Ross remembered; her eyes started to tear up as she was talking about her sister. Ross divulged; he didn't have any siblings. His parents split up when he was nine and he ended up living with his mom.

"She died three years back from breast cancer. She was my hero, raised me all by herself." His dad remarried and had another family. He told her; his job is his wife right now. Looking at Jade, he thought, she was beautiful both inside and out. She was soft spoken and articulate when she spoke. He couldn't take his eye off her beautiful derriere when she was walking to the ladies room during dinner. Those jeans were made for her. Her legs went on forever.

Shapiro was still on the phone when Ross indicated to him that he was going to look at the victim's appointment book. He wanted to look at the dates the victim wanted to switch with Kim Marshall.

Ross determined the victim had an appointment scheduled at ten p.m. on each of these days at the Savoy Hotel. This is the why Skylar needed to switch her night shifts with Kim.

Shapiro got off the phone, "you got something" he asked Ross.

"When I spoke to the victim's best friend, she explained Skylar left a message a week ago, asking for shift changes. The victim needed day shifts. Looking at her appointment book, now I know why. She had appointments late in the evening at the Savoy Hotel," Ross said.

Ross told Shapiro about Kim supposedly leaving Skylar a message the day after she received Skylar's message. Shapiro knew Kim was lying. "There were no messages on her cell phone, but I'll check with Levi to make sure." Shapiro said. Pino Levi was the computer specialist. He dealt with digital evidence.

"The Savoy, wow that's big bucks. How can someone on a nurse's salary afford the Savoy Hotel?" Shapiro said.

"We need to find out what she was doing at these hotels. I have a pretty good idea of what she was doing," Ross said. Shapiro concurred.

"I'll speak with the General Manager of the Savoy Hotel tomorrow."

"How did it go with the intern?" Ross asked.

"Oh, he's a real piece of work. He didn't want to speak with me because he thought it would interfere with his internship. I made it very clear to him that he could answer questions here or at the station and if he still chose not to answer, he would be arrested for impeding a homicide investigation. He quickly changed his tune. The victim's death didn't seem to frazzle him. He was more worried about himself. Guy was really cold. He admitted to sleeping with the victim. They were just having fun. He was working at the hospital at the time of the resident's death. I checked him out. Born in Hamilton in 1995, never been arrested, not even a speeding ticket. He completed his medical degree through McMaster University in Hamilton and is completing his residency in emergency medicine at Holy Angels Hospital. I'm going to check out his alibi though. Apparently, he's under the supervision of Dr. Rodney Martins during his residency. You should have seen the worry in his eyes when I told him, either myself or my partner, would be speaking with his supervisor. I think he pissed himself."

Ross' phone rang. It was Dr. Lind. "Hey doc, you still working?

"I was just about to go home but I wanted to let you know there was no DNA on the rope used to bind the victim's wrists and ankles. The blood and epithelial cells belonged to the victim. The clothing she was wearing is still being examined. He must have worn gloves. Toxicology yielded a small amount of chloroform in her system. This kept her sedated or was used to abduct her so she wouldn't put up a fight. She must have ingested or inhaled it because I found no needle marks. That's it. Wish I could have given you better news."

"Thanks Doc."

Ross let Shapiro know about the findings or lack there of.

"How about you keep up with the hotel General Managers and financial records and I 'll speak with Dr. Martins," Ross suggested to Shapiro.

Shapiro nodded, "sounds good." He left to go home to his wife. Ross completed reports until midnight and then finally left to go home.

It was almost midnight. Jade was tired. She was lying in bed, thinking of Detective Ross. She was attracted to him, and she had a feeling, he was interested in her. She thought, bad timing, just her luck. The last thing she should be thinking about is a man. Her sister had been murdered two days ago and rather than crying over her, here she is falling for the cop who is investigating her death. Jade was cried out. Detective Ross was supportive and kind. She needed that right now. He had a dry sense of humor and a great laugh. He was a very handsome man. Tall, with lean hips, beautiful green eyes, dark wavy hair cut short, strong jaw line and olive skin tone, which made his straight teeth look even whiter. His smile was gorgeous. Five o'clock shadow on his face that made him look even more sexier than he was.

"Stop, give your head a shake," she said to herself. This is insane. She needed to stay focused.

CHAPTER 6

THEY FOUND HER BODY. WELL good for them. She was nothing but a slut. She paid dearly for what I saw the night I followed her to the Windsor Park Hotel. She took a cab to the hotel. She didn't even look like herself. She had on a blond wig and way too much makeup for his taste. The dress she was wearing didn't leave much to the imagination. I saw her going into the hotel to do God knows what. I knew what she was doing. I waited until she came out a couple of hours later. She came out with "him." She had been with "him." Blood boiled in his veins. He wanted to kill them both, but it was her he hated more. She won't be with him anymore. She got what she deserved. She fooled everybody including him. That slut.

Shapiro had come and gone from the station. He left a message saying he was going to speak with the General Manager of the Savoy Hotel. He also let Ross know they were waiting on the financial records right now.

Ross needed to verify the intern's alibi. He was heading to the hospital. While driving, he wondered; how Jade was doing today.

Ross arrived at the hospital. He walked into the emergency department and asked to speak to Dr. Rodney Martins. The ward clerk explained he was in with a patient at the moment.

"That's fine, please let him know I'm here and will wait for him."

Ross saw, who he believed to be Dr. Martins come out of a patient's room and went to the nursing desk. There he was told that a Detective was waiting for him. He signed off on paperwork and began walking towards Detective Ross. Dr. Martins appeared to be in his late thirties. He was of average height, thin, and nonathletic. He appeared to be an introvert. He had brown, medium length, wavy hair, wore glasses, and looked professional, wearing a stethoscope around his neck. Nothing really stood out about this man. His lab coat had his name embroidered on it.

"Detective Ross, I understand you wish to speak to me."

"That's right Dr. Martins. Do you have a couple of minutes? I'd like to ask you some questions."

"Of course, lets go somewhere more private."

Ross followed him to a private room with a cot where he believed doctors caught some sleep when shifts became long.

"What is this about detective?" Dr. Martins asked."

"I am investigating the murder of Skylar Rose. She was a registered nurse in the emergency department. She was found dead three days ago."

"Yes, yes, I did hear about that. Such a tragedy. I didn't know her well. We didn't work together very often."

"I questioned your intern, Morgan Sinclair, yesterday. I need to know if he was working at the hospital four days ago?"

Dr. Martins was surprised. "May I ask why?" Ross repeated himself, without answering the question.

"Well let me look at my schedule." He took out his cell phone and looked at his schedule.

"Morgan Sinclair was working because I was working. Because I am his supervisor, he works the same shifts I do. Morgan, I mean Dr. Sinclair, did an eighteen-hour shift that day."

"So, you were here as well for eighteen hours?"

"I was here before Dr. Sinclair came in. I was catching up on sleep, in this very room. When I woke up, he had already signed off on three patients. We've been working short lately and the emergency department is always busy, so we sleep whenever we can. The interns and hospitalists are an immense help to us. Dr. Sinclair needs a supervisor to work with who is a licensed physician. He can't work alone until he becomes a full-fledged doctor."

"How long has he been an intern at this hospital Dr. Martins?"

"He's been here just over three months. Residency is typically twelve months."

"Have you noticed any problems or issues with Dr. Sinclair," Ross asked.

"None. Thus far he has exhibited excellent assessment skills for diagnosing, as well as critical thinking skills. The only con is that he can be cold when speaking with patients. He needs to be more compassionate in my opinion."

"How long have you been here Dr. Martins?"

"I did my residency here as well. I have been a practicing physician here for about ten years."

Ross made notes in his little black book and thanked Dr. Martins for his time. Ross thought, another dead end. Hope Shapiro is doing better with the footage.

Shapiro spoke to Marcus Cruz this morning. The General Manager of the Savoy Hotel explained it will take time to get the footage together. Meanwhile, the footage from the Windsor Park Hotel was sent over to the station via courier, the day before. Shapiro had gone over the footage from the dates and times indicated in the victim's appointment book twice and couldn't find anything. What was he missing? Why can't I see her? Were the dates and times, correct?

"Hey Shapiro'" Adam Mc Allister, another detective called out, "here are the financials on the Rose case." He just dropped everything on Shapiro's desk. Shapiro was examining the victim's financial record, when he made a sound that sounded like a whistle. He couldn't believe what he was seeing. He thought, for a nurse she was making more than a doctor would probably be making. Ross is going to love this. As he continued to look at the files, Pino Levi called from upstairs.

"Shapiro, I double checked and got nothing from the victim's computer. She was emailing her sister and friends. The content shows nothing illegal or shady. She's done online shopping, nothing expensive. She was however looking at real estate and cars. Maybe she was thinking of buying a house or a new car. With regards to the cell phone, there was nothing out of the ordinary. No messages or texts. I checked the numbers, and she called her sister, the hospital, and her friend Kim often. However, there were two numbers that belonged to burner phones, and I can't trace those numbers. That's all I got.'

Shapiro thanked him for the information.

Five days after her body was discovered, Jade had her sister cremated. She wanted peace for her sister. She had chosen a brilliant butterfly urn in a beautiful lavender color. Jade remembered; Skylar loved butterflies. Their bright colors and their elegance and grace when they flew. The engraving on the urn had read "My Sister, My Best Friend."

"My dear are you alright?" Mr. Barnes asked.

"I'm just so sad. I can't believe my little sister's gone. My hearts broken and I feel so alone. When our parents died, we had each other. Now, I'm really alone." Jade began crying.

"Can I call someone for you? You shouldn't be by yourself."

"No thank you, I'll be fine. Thank you for your kindness, Mr. Barnes. Would it be alright if my sister's ashes be kept here, until I am ready to leave Sudbury and go home? I feel my sister's ashes would be safer here rather than at the hotel."

"Of course, my dear. That would be fine. Please let me know when you are ready to pick up your sister's ashes."

"I will. Thanks again." Jade quickly left as she started crying again.

CHAPTER 7

ROSS FINALLY GOT BACK TO the station. He updated the information he obtained about this murder case in the Major Case Management (MCM) system which helped police identify common links in crimes committed in different locations in Ontario- crimes that might have been committed by the same person. There wasn't much information to add as he had hit dead ends at every turn. The software was a useful tool for solving certain crimes such as homicides. Shapiro had also updated the system with his information.

Ross was thinking about Jade and how she was feeling. He would call her later. He noticed Shapiro was concentrating on something.

"What are you so focused on? It must be interesting." Ross said.

"Oh, it is." Shapiro said. He was smiling. "Our victim's financials are very interesting. She was banking six to eight thousand dollars a month, on top of her wage at the hospital. She would deposit at least two thousand dollars cash, one to two days after each appointment. There were no cashed cheques or deposits made by a third party. She was doing more than nursing."

"That's interesting. Let's call a spade a spade, shall we. This girl was a high-priced call girl that only the rich could afford. How does a nurse by day moonlight as a call girl by night? How does she recruit clients, or do they recruit her?"

"Oh, that reminds me, Levi from upstairs found nothing on her computer or cell phone. He found two phone numbers that were each called twice in the last two months. Levi called both numbers that went dead. They were burner phones. Whoever was calling, was careful or perhaps, our victim was being careful." Shapiro added.

Ross wondered how well Jade really knew her sister. "You know, Jade talks about her like an innocent angel. She needs to know what we found out. Maybe she could shed some light on what was really going on. I need to speak to her."

"You like her. I see the way you look at her. She's a beautiful woman," Shapiro said. "Be careful. She isn't going to take the news well. She's vulnerable right now."

Ross didn't want to hurt Jade, but he knew he was going to. She would end up probably hating him. He picked up his jacket and left to go see her. He called her to let her know he was coming over to speak to her.

Shapiro watched him leave. His phone rang. He could see the call was transferred from central intake. He picked it up, identifying himself "this is Detective Shapiro."

"Detective Shapiro, my name is Hal Jenkins. I own Jenkins Auto Repair on the Kingsway. My employees heard on the news the police are looking for a burgundy Malibu belonging to the murdered female found in the park three days ago."

"That's correct Mr. Jenkins."

"Its in my shop as we speak. Its been here for the last week."

Shapiro grabbed his jacket, while letting Jenkins know he was on his way. He knew where the shop was. He made a point of calling Ross to let him know he had a lead on the victim's car.

It was three o'clock by the time Shapiro got to the auto repair shop. It was a busy place, and it was noisy due to bolt blasters and spinners, powered wrenches, pressure testing kits, vacuum pumps, and all the other tools mechanics use. Cars were lifted in two bays while mechanics worked underneath them. The mechanics wore full body overalls with their names embroidered on them and the company name as well. Ross approached the older gentleman at the counter that was nicely dressed in a navy-blue polo shirt and a pair of jeans, assuming it was Jenkins, and he was right. Shapiro identified himself and presented his badge. Jenkins showed him the car. Shapiro checked it out and confirmed it was the victim's car. The licence plate matched. There was a nursing uniform in the back seat.

"Did anybody touch anything in the car?" Shapiro asked.

"She came in to have her brakes changed. The steering wheel, shifter and accelerator should have been the only things touched, besides the brakes, of course."

Shapiro was curious, "police have been looking for the car for the last four days, why are you just calling me now Mr. Jenkins? Was she alone when she brought the car in?"

"I just got back to work today after a week of being away. My wife had a cardiac procedure performed in Toronto. She's got a ticker that beats erratically. My employees didn't know what to do. They waited for me to come back. According to the employees, she came in alone and left alone. The boys, my mechanics remembered her. Said she was a real looker."

"When was she told to pick up the car?" Shapiro asked.

"She was told it was busy here and brake parts needed to be ordered. The young lady told my office assistant Mandy she would call in a couple of days to find out exactly when her car would be fixed, but according to Mandy, she never did."

Shapiro wanted to question Mandy. "Is Mandy here right now?"

"She sure is. She's in the office. Come with me." Jenkins said.

Shapiro followed Jenkins into the office and was introduced to Mandy. She was a young girl, maybe twenty years old, wore no makeup and her hair was pulled up in a ponytail. She was sitting behind a desk, looking at a computer, while speaking with someone on the phone. Jenkins introduced Detective Shapiro to Mandy.

"Have I done something wrong? She wouldn't make eye contact.

Shapiro reassured her, she had not. Shapiro wanted to know how the victim sounded the day she spoke with her.

"She was happy her car was being fixed. She said she was looking at other cars cause her car was always breaking down and she was fed up." Mandy explained.

"Thank you, Mandy." Shapiro walked out of the office and called to have the car brought in so it could be processed for any possible evidence.

Shapiro was wondering how she got around without her car. Did she need it? Was someone giving her rides, or did she borrow someone's car? Shapiro knew she had taken the week off. So, what did she use to get around during that week?

Ross got to the hotel and stopped short of knocking on Jade's door. He knew this would be another blow to her. He knocked on the door. Jade opened the door. She was dressed in a baby blue sweat suit. She had no make up on and her hair was in a long braid. Even dressed casually, she was beautiful, Ross thought.

"Detective Ross, is everything alright? When you called you sounded so serious. I didn't know how to take it. Has something happened? Do you have any leads on who killed my sister?"

Ross knew there was no easy way to say this, so he was just going to say it. "Jade when we searched your sister's apartment, we found items suggesting your sister was leading a double life."

"What? What are you talking about? A double life. My sister would have told me. That's ridiculous."

"Are you sure about that Jade? Maybe you didn't know her as well as you thought you did.

"Excuse me detective. My sister and I were very close. She would have told me what she was doing."

"We found items suggesting that she was…. she was…." Ross was having a tough time with this. It wasn't like him. He was usually more professional than this.

"Come out with it, tell me about this double life." Jade was shaking, she was so upset. She didn't need this.

"We have evidence to suggest that your sister was working as a high-priced escort."

"What! That's utterly ridiculous. Your evidence is wrong. This is crazy. Skylar would never do anything like that. Sisters talk. She would have told me. She wasn't a call girl. She was a registered nurse. There has to be another explanation for the evidence you found." By now Jade was crying and shaking.

"I'm sorry Jade the evidence isn't wrong and there is no other explanation, that we've found. We found tens of thousands of dollars in her bank account. Did she inherit any money that you know of? How do you explain the money?"

"She's been working a lot of overtime, which might explain the money."

"Not that kind of money Jade."

Jade was still crying. "When was she supposedly working as an escort? She was always at the hospital."

"The majority of appointments were scheduled for Fridays and Saturdays, late in the evening. Her boss at work told me that she was starting to call in sick more often. Her supervisor believed she was burning the candle at both ends. She was always tired. She also stated that Skylar wasn't taking overtime in the last couple of months."

Jade looked up at Ross as if a light had gone off in her head. She surprised herself. She stopped crying and composed herself.

"What is it, Jade? What do you want to tell me? If you know something you have to tell me." Ross demanded.

"I would ask her to come and visit on weekends she was off work, but she always said she was working overtime. She'd say that if I let her know sooner, she wouldn't have taken the overtime. There were weekends that I wanted to visit but she was always busy with work or school assignments. Looking back now, she was just making excuses." Ross told her, there was nothing on her computer to suggest she was taken on-line courses.

Jade was now sobbing. Ross moved closer and touched her shoulders with both hands, to face her. She moved in closer to him, resting her head on his chest, still crying. Ross held her until she stopped crying. She lifted her head off his chest and looked up at him. They were a couple inches apart from each other. Ross wanted to taste those beautiful lips, but he pushed away and gently let go of her. He knew she was hurting. This wasn't right. He was developing feelings for her. He needed to be professional about this.

Jade composed herself. She felt foolish. She moved away, turning her back to Ross and walked to the window. She was staring outside when she said "regardless of what my sister did or didn't do, what she was or wasn't, she didn't deserve to die the way she did. I want her killer found."

"I'm sorry Jade, I didn't come here to hurt you. We are going to find out who did this."

Jade didn't turn around. She just kept staring out the window. She was in her own little world. She didn't even hear Ross leave the room. She turned around when she heard the door close and began to cry.

CHAPTER 8

IT WAS THE EARLY PART of the evening and Ross was at home. His home was a one-bedroom apartment, in Garson. It was simple, but clean. There was nothing special about it. The walls were beige with browns and rust colors. There was hardly anything in the fridge. He was rarely at home. He didn't want to go back to the station after his encounter with Jade earlier. He knew he hurt her. He wanted to kiss her. He needed to leave, or he was going to take her in his arms, lay her down on the bed and get lost in her all night. He thought, while holding her earlier, she was so warm and soft. Her breast pressed against his chest felt wonderful, and when she looked at him, standing so close, those blue eyes were piercing, even though she had been crying. He wanted this woman more than he has wanted anything or anyone in this life.

His thoughts of Jade were interrupted when he heard his cell phone ringing. He didn't want to answer it, but he knew he had to. Caller ID indicated it was Shapiro. He called to tell him the victim's car gave them nothing.

"Technicians found nothing. She really covered her tracks." Shapiro said with frustration.

"You're right. I think its time to pressure her friend, Kim. I know she knows more, and I know she has been lying. I'm going to confront her on that so-called message she left and see how she reacts."

"How did it go with Jade?"

"Not good. She can't believe her sister was having sex for money. She remembers her sister being a sweet girl and doesn't want to think of her in any other way, especially in a negative way. When I left, she was just staring out the window. I'm going to give her some time."

"We'll see what Kim has to say. I'm going with you. Double pressure is a good thing. Get some sleep." Shapiro hung up.

It was the weekend. Both Ross and Shapiro were putting in overtime this weekend, to catch up on paperwork and look at the hotel footage. They wanted to speak to Kim Marshall first, so they showed up at her place, early in the morning. They wanted to catch her off guard. They thought if she's not home, they would go to the hospital. Ross knocked on the door twice and she answered the door yawning. They had woken her up. She was surprised to see Detective Ross and who she assumed was his partner.

"Ms. Marshall, you remember me, and this is my partner, Detective Shapiro. May we come in? We have more questions."

"Its early in the morning. I don't know how else I can help, but come in."

"You can start by telling us the truth. You lied to me when you said that you left Ms. Rose a message. There was no message found on her cell phone, so you either didn't leave her one or you left it on another phone. You also lied about Ms. Rose not calling in sick more often and taking more overtime. Your supervisor, Ms. Lasalle already confirmed she was calling in sick more than usual and she had stopped taking overtime."

Ross and Shapiro were coming up short every time they turned around with this case. They were tired of it.

"Your best friend was murdered. Start telling the truth Ms. Marshall. We can talk here, or we can go down to the station. If you know something, you need to tell us. Am I making myself clear, Ms. Marshall?" Ross said.

Kim was stunned. She looked at both of them for a while. She knew she had to tell them the truth, but she had made a promise to her friend and didn't want to betray her trust, even if she was gone.

She remembers Skylar saying, "you can't tell anyone. Promise me Kim."

"Ms. Marshall, we know about the late-night visits to expensive hotels, the blonde wigs, the money, expensive clothing, and other items. Was she having sex for money with rich clients? You need to tell us what you know."

They could tell she was rolling things around in her head. She was weighing something heavy on her shoulders. She walked into the living room, sat down on the sofa, looked at a photo of her and Skylar, which was on the end table and started crying. She picked up the glass frame that housed it and was touching the photo of her friend, with her forefinger.

"Skylar was my best friend. I loved her like a sister. She told me that she had found a way to make a lot of money. More money than she would make nursing at the hospital. She would come here to get ready to meet whoever she was meeting, leave her car here and take a taxi to the hotels. Then she would take a taxi back and pick up her car. She would take her wig off in the car and remove her make-up as well, before going home. She didn't want to leave her apartment looking the way she did for one of her "appointments," nor did she want to be seen once she got back to her place. She had nosy neighbours."

"How did she become involved in being a high-priced escort? Where did she recruit clients? Do you know who these clients were?" Ross asked.

Kim was still crying, holding the photo of her and her friend. "When I asked her that, she explained that about seven months ago, when we were at a bar with friends, a woman approached her while in the bathroom, thought Skylar was beautiful and told her to give her a call if she wanted to make some real money. The woman gave Skylar, her phone number. Skylar wanted some excitement in her life. I could tell she was getting bored. When we were in college, she would drive to Toronto on Saturday morning to strip at a club Saturday night and drive back home Sunday. She made more money in that one night than I did working part-time at the drug store, all month. I was the only one that knew. She never told her sister. She knew her sister wouldn't approve."

Ross thought, if Jade knew this, it would kill her. Jade wouldn't believe it.

Ms. Marshall interrupted his thoughts, "when Jade was over here the day after Skylar was killed, I knew she was looking for answers. I didn't want to talk about Skylar, because I was afraid, I would somehow give away her secret and what she was doing, so all I talked about was everything else. She must have thought I was an awful person."

"Do you know who this woman was from the bar? Had you seen her before somewhere else?

"No idea who she was. I hadn't seen her before and before you ask, I don't have her phone number. Skylar only told me about what she was doing two months later. She was having a good time. This woman hooked her up with men that were very successful and demanded discretion. She didn't give me any names. She did hint that there were only two or three men that requested her services. Skylar would make a thousand to twelve hundred dollars an hour and was paid in cash. She would see them a couple of times a month, for a couple of hours, but I don't know who they are. She would call me the next day after one of her "appointments" so I wouldn't worry about her."

"How did she contact these men? We found nothing out of the ordinary on her cell phone."

Kim explained, her clients would use burner phones so the phones couldn't be traced. The men provided the phones.

"Is there anything else you can tell us Ms. Marshall?"

"No, I've told you everything I know. Do you think what she was doing got her killed? She was happy. She wouldn't be doing it if she felt scared or it put her in danger. Skylar was thinking of going part-time at the hospital. She had all these plans."

"We can't answer that. We don't have all the pieces to the puzzle at this point." Shapiro explained.

"If there is anything else you can think of, please call either myself or Detective Shapiro." Ross provided his card, along with Shapiro's.

Kim made a point of telling them one last thing. "Perhaps, what Skylar was doing may have been wrong to others. Some people would have thought of her as someone who had no respect for herself or was immoral for having sex for money, with men she barely knew. People always talk and judge others, without looking at their own lives because they would see they're not so perfect after all. Skylar was a compassionate person. She loved life. She enjoyed life. She loved her friends, and she adored her sister. She was a great nurse. She believed in working smart not hard. What's wrong with that? Regardless, of what people thought, no one has the right to take someone's life because they don't agree or like what that person is doing. Who ever killed Skylar, made themselves judge and jury."

"One last question, Ms. Marshall, when was the last time you actually saw the victim?"

"Six days ago, when she brought my car back. She was using my care cause hers was in the shop. It needed new brakes; I think."

They both left Kim Marshall deflated. They went over the information provided by her in the car. It was interesting. To look at the victim's photo, it was hard to picture her as a high-priced escort or stripper, for that matter. Sometimes you really don't know people, Ross thought.

"I'm thinking lawyers, doctors, judges, politicians. What do you think?" Shapiro asked Ross.

"I think we need to take a closer look at the hotel footage." Ross answered.

Jade woke up feeling empty. She had a really bad headache, was cold and clammy. She wasn't feeling well at all. She hadn't eaten since yesterday mid-afternoon. All she could think about was what Detective Ross had told her about Skylar. "He must have it all wrong," she said to herself. Skylar wouldn't do something that involved sex for money. Why would she? She had a respectable job, that she could be proud of, she thought. She really felt dizzy now. She could barely stand and when she tried, she passed out.

Jade woke up in the hospital. Her eyes were trying to focus, and she was weak when she tried to speak. She noticed Kim hanging a small IV bag.

"What happened? "Her voice groggy and her mouth was dry.

"Hotel housekeeping found you passed out in your room and called an ambulance. You were dehydrated and your blood sugar was dangerously low. You needed fluids and sugar. The doctor ordered dextrose with water. This won't take long. You'll feel better soon. You were given medication when you came in and this is the last of it. Jade, when was the last time you ate?" Kim asked.

"What time is it?

"Its close to noon."

"The last time I ate was yesterday afternoon. I had a dreadful day yesterday."

"Sorry to hear that. I miss Skylar, but I can't imagine the pain your going through." Kim was concerned about her.

Jade didn't answer. She just laid on the emergency room gurney and closed her eyes.

"Ms. Rose, how are you feeling?" Dr. Martins asked.

"Better, thank you."

"That's wonderful. Detective Ross will be picking you up in the next couple of hours."

"What? Why? That won't be necessary. I can call a cab to get back to the hotel." Jade was irritated.

"You were weak and very lethargic when you came in. It would be unethical of me to send you home alone, Ms. Rose. Nurse Marshall explained that you are not from here and besides her, she doesn't know of anyone else, you would know to escort you back to your hotel. She mentioned Detective Ross, so I called him."

Jade didn't say anything, just sighed and closed her eyes again.

"Ms. Rose, I am terribly sorry about your sister. This must be hard for you. Do you require anything temporarily to help you sleep? I can prescribe something for you, Dr. Martins asked.

"No thank you Dr. Martins. I'll be fine."

Jade closed her eyes and fell asleep. She was tired.

Ross and Shapiro had just got back to the station and were just about to start looking at hotel footage when Dr. Martins called Ross. "She's where? What happened to her? Is she alright? I'll be there in a couple of hours. Let her rest."

Shapiro could see concern all over Ross' face.

When Ross hung up, Shapiro asked, "what was that about?"

"That was Dr. Martins telling me that Jade was brought into the ER by ambulance. Apparently, housekeeping found her passed out, in her room. He told me she was feeling much better, but couldn't tell me what was wrong with her, due to confidentiality reasons. She would have to tell me herself. He needs me to pick her up. He won't let her leave by herself. Kim Marshall gave him my name and number. Kim couldn't think of anyone else, and her shift ends at seven p.m."

"Well, you go pick up Jade and I'll get a head start on the footage. I only have like ten hours of footage to go through unless I go blind first." Shapiro joked.

"I owe you big. I'll be back as soon as I can."

Shapiro laughed, "Sure, you will."

It was two thirty p.m. Ross parked the car as close as he could to the emergency department doors. He walked in and went to the desk. One of the nurses at the desk asked, "how can I help you." He explained he was here to pick up Jade Rose. "She is in examining room nine. Please wait here.

"Detective Ross," he heard Dr. Martins calling. "She's much better but angry at me for calling you. Please come with me."

As soon as Ross saw her, he just wanted to hold her. She looked so fragile. She was pale and withdrawn. She was still wearing her pyjamas. "I'm here to take you back to the hotel. How are you feeling?"

She felt so embarrassed. "I'm fine. I don't need a babysitter. You don't need to take me back; I'll just grab a cab."

"Perhaps, I didn't make myself clear Ms. Rose," Dr. Martins interjected. "If you want to leave the hospital, you will need Detective Ross to escort you back. You're still weak."

Ross was very firm when he said "no worries, I'll make sure she gets back to the hotel, and I'll stay with her until she feels better. I'll make sure she eats and drinks." Jade knew he meant it and wasn't going to put up with any of her crap.

As Ross and Jade were leaving, Kim Marshall approached them. "Jade, you take good care and if you need anything, call me."

"Thanks Kim." Jade just wanted to leave.

By the time they left the hospital it was close to four p.m. Dr. Martins explained that if she continued to feel sick, she should return to the ER. There was no way Jade was going back to the ER. She felt fine. The ride back to the hotel was a silent one. Neither one of them spoke. Ross knew Jade was angry with him for what he had said to her, about her sister. He parked the car close to the entrance of the hotel, got out, and rounded the car to help Jade out. The hospital had given her a robe to cover up with. He helped her up and walked her inside. As they were walking across the bright lobby, Jade was thankful it wasn't busy. She was so embarrassed. Julie, the front desk clerk smiled, "glad to see you're back Ms. Rose. Hope you're feel better."

"Thank you" is all Jade said, she just wanted to get back to her room. Ross escorted her to her room, she held on to his arm and walked without any difficulty. He opened the door, and she sat down in the recliner provided in the room. Then he left to go and park his car in the hotel parking area. He had taken the hotel key. He wanted to make sure Jade was fine, so he was going to stay for a while. As he was crossing the lobby to get back to the room, the hotel manager stopped him to ask about Jade. He explained she's fine and just needs to eat. He entered the room to find Jade was in the shower. The bathroom door wasn't shut all the way, it was left ajar. As he took off his jacket, he thought of Jade nude, lathering up a loofa sponge and washing her body with it, over her breasts, her beautiful ass, and long legs. He heard the water shut off.

Jade came out of the bathroom, with a towel wrapped around her head and covered with a light pink terry cloth robe, down to just above her knees. "You don't have to stay detective, I'll be fine. I needed a shower. I feel like a new person."

Ross could see the color coming back to her face. He was happy she was feeling better.

Jade was standing at the end of the bed, when Ross stirred in the chair, he was sitting in. He didn't want to move to close to her because he didn't trust himself. He wanted to take that robe off and see all of her. He wanted this woman so bad, it hurt. He's wanted her from the first time he saw her, he thought.

"I know you'll be fine. Look Jade, I wanted to talk to you about last night. I didn't want to hurt you, but obviously I did, and you ended up in the hospital."

"Detective I'm not angry with you, I'm angry at myself. You were just doing your job and being honest with me. I guess, I just didn't want to hear it. I didn't want to think of my little sister having sex for money. I remember a sweet girl, who was so happy when she graduated with a nursing degree. I forgot about the free spirit she was and the trouble she got into with boys, when she was a teenager. She would break curfew, at times she wouldn't come home till morning and other times she would tell my parents she was staying over at a friends place, when she was with some guy all night. My parents worst nightmare was their youngest daughter coming home and telling them she was pregnant, or not coming home at all. I thought she had gotten all that out of her system. Obviously, Skylar did what she wanted to do. The last few years, we hardly saw each other and even when we spoke on the phone, the conversations were short. I realize now, I really didn't know my sister at all." As Jade was talking, she took the towel off her head and Ross saw beautiful long wavy wet brown hair fall to her waist. She was exquisite, he thought.

"People change and you don't always know what a person is really like, even if they are blood related. Skylar did her own thing and didn't ask anyone for permission." Ross said.

"I know, I just wished she would have trusted me enough to tell me what she was doing. She was an adult who made her own decisions. I didn't need to know, I guess."

Ross just looked at her. "Your sister was lucky to have you, Jade. You need to stop thinking that she didn't trust you because she did. She probably didn't tell you because she genuinely cared about what you thought of her but didn't care about what anybody else thought of her. Don't do this to yourself, your going to make yourself sick again. You need to rest. Can I get you anything to eat or drink? You need to keep your strength up or you'll be back in the hospital"

"Detective, there's another reason I'm angry at my self." Jade just looked at him. "I just lost my sister and all I can think about is you."

Ross just stared at her. He couldn't believe what she just said. His focus now was solely on her and nothing else.

"When you were here last night, I wanted you to kiss me. I didn't want you to leave. I wanted you to stay with me and not because I was vulnerable but because I wanted you." Jade admitted.

Ross didn't waste anytime, he stood up out of the chair and moved closer to her, now standing inches away from her. He could smell the sweet scent of vanilla. He looked into those beautiful blue eyes, caressed her shoulders, looked at her lips and pulled her to him. He kissed her with such intensity, he could barely breath. Her lips parted, and his tongue tasted hers. He broke the kiss. They were both breathing heavy.

He wrapped his arms around her, whispering in her ear, "I've wanted you from the moment I saw you." She looked at him and touched his face.

Ross looked at her again, he couldn't get enough of her beautiful face. Their eyes were locked on each other.

His hands moved to the tie keeping her robe from falling open, "are you sure about this Jade? You just go out to the hospital."

"I'm fine. I've been sure about this since I met you. I don't want to wait any longer."

Ross undid the tie around her robe and opened up her robe, allowing it to fall to the floor. He moved back a step and took her all in.

"You're beautiful Jade Rose. Absolutely gorgeous." He gently guided her back to the bed and she laid down on it. He was watching her, while he undressed. He was all male, Jade thought. He came down on her and kissed her for a long time, then moved down to her neck and abdomen. Her skin was so soft. Mark touched her warm moist sex. She was moaning with pleasure. He fondled her breasts, before taking a nipple in his mouth. Jade groaned louder.

He looked at her and quickly put a condom on and mounted her. He penetrated her and began moving in and out slowly.

"You have no idea how good your feel Jade." She was moaning, finding pleasure in the way he filled her. He lowered himself to her and kissed her again, while moving faster now, wanting her to find her release. He knew it was time. She was moaning, breathing heavy and finally cried out in ecstasy.

His release came with such potency, that his whole body shook. He was breathing so hard, looking down at her and she up at him. They were both glistening with moisture.

"That was wonderful," she said.

"I hope I didn't hurt you."

"No, I'm fine, Detective Ross.

"That's good. Next time were going to take things slower. I want to enjoy every inch of you. I can't get enough of you."

"Next time," Jade prodded.

"Most definitely, there's going to be a next time and I'm going to take my time with you. By the way, I think you can call me Mark, after this."

They were both laughing. They decided to stay in for dinner and called for room service. Ross made sure Jade ate. She was going to need all her strength for what he had planned.

CHAPTER 9

ROSS WOKE UP LOOKING AT Jade still sleeping. They had sex twice after dinner and it was great. He can't get enough of this woman. She was gentle, yet strong. She looked like an angel. Her breathing was quiet and even. Her hair was tousled all over the pillow. It was so sexy. She was so sexy. He knew every inch of her body and kissed every inch of her body. She was delicious. They were all over the bed devouring each other.

Jade was starting to wake up. "You're up already?" She said with her eyes partially closed.

"I've got to go to work Jade. I need to shower first and then swing by my place to change my clothes."

"Will I see you today?" Jade thought she sounded needy.

"I'll call you later. I still need to solve your sister's murder.

"Of course. Sometimes I just want to forget."

He kissed her and got into the shower.

Ross was at the station within forty-five minutes. Shapiro came in shortly after him. He noticed Ross staring out at nothing.

'Everything alright? How's Jade? I didn't call you yesterday. I figured you had your hands full.

"Thanks. Jade is great. She's wonderful. I'm the one that's an idiot."

Shapiro just looked at him with curiosity. He would want an explanation for that comment, but it would have to wait.

"I found our victim in the footage from the Windsor Park Hotel. When I looked at the footage the first time, I was looking for the victim, the way she normally looked. Then I remembered the wigs and dresses, so I started all over again."

Shapiro sat at his computer and went right to the footage. "Come here, I'll show you. Here she is in one of the three times you see her, according to her appointment book. I had to go back a half hour, prior to the appointment times. She shows up early for her appointments. She leaves approximately two to three hours later."

"She doesn't look anything like herself. What a transformation." Ross pointed out.

"I know. That's why I missed her the first time I went through the footage. When I showed her picture around to the hotel employees, they didn't seem to recognize her. Mind you I was there during the day. I think I may have better luck with the evening or night shift employees."

"Can I see the footage of her according to the other dates and times?" Ross asked.

Shapiro showed his partner the rest of the footage. The victim knew exactly what she was doing. You could tell, she knew how to work it. She was gorgeous and graceful. She was about the same height as Jade. She was curvier so she looked like a goddess in those dresses. No man could keep his eyes off her. When she walked, she was confident. Ross thought.

Ross was curious. "Who is the gentleman that has his arm around her? Do we know who he is? You can barely see his face. It seems like he knows exactly where the cameras are and is purposely trying to avoid them."

"I have no idea. I will be asking Mr. Hopkins. He might know." Shapiro said.

"I hope he does know something. Did the footage come in from the Savoy Hotel?"

"I'll tell you in one minute." Shapiro saw the courier coming in, needing a signature for the package he was carrying. "Hey, I think that's for me." Sure, enough it was. It was the footage from the Savoy Hotel.

"When I asked you how Jade was, I was surprised by your answer." What was that all about? Did something happen?"

"Oh, you can say that. It hit me this morning, that she's leaving to go back to the Sault, and I can't seem to think about anything or anyone else, except for her. I need to stay away from her. I think its best for both of us."

"She's going to hate you for hurting her. Take it from someone who has been married a long time. You can control and change your behaviour, but you can't control the way you feel about something or someone. Eventually, your feelings are going to take you over."

"I think I'm in big trouble," Ross admitted.

Shapiro got up. "Let's go talk to Hopkins." A picture of the blonde Skylar was printed. They needed to speak to the employees again and show them this new picture. They needed to catch a break on this case. Its been almost a week and nothing, except the footage. They both got up and headed for the exit.

It took almost twenty minutes to get to the Windsor Park Hotel due to morning rush hour. Both Shapiro and Ross walked to the front desk. Ross noticed the richness of this hotel. Grey marble floors and a frond desk in the centre of the lobby. The lobby was elegantly decorated with a waiting area on either side of the front desk. Directly in the centre of the tall ceiling was a large and beautiful chandelier that sparkled as it moved. The waiting areas were decorated in various shades of blues and grays. The plush sofas were a Robin's egg blue and the accent chairs beside them were shades of blue with hints of light yellows. There were six windows which let in beautiful natural light, and it was lavished with beautiful healthy plants. Everyone had a uniform on but were different depending on what position they held, and every employee had a name tag on.

"We're here to see Mr. Hopkins."

"I remember you, Detective Shapiro. I will let him know you're here." Hector said.

"Thank you, Hector." Shapiro remembered him from the front desk.

"Detective Shapiro, nice to see you again."

Mr. Hopkins was a middle-aged man. He was a fairly large man of average height who carried his weight well. He was balding on top and clean shaven. His navy-blue suit was professional looking and there were no wrinkles on his white shirt. He had a matching tie, and his black loafers were shiny and expensive.

"How can I be of assistance detective?"

"Good morning Mr. Hopkins. Thank you for seeing us. This is my partner, Detective Ross."

Both men shook hands. Shapiro pulled out the picture of Skylar with the blonde wig and presented it to Mr. Hopkins.

"Have you ever seen this young lady in the hotel?"

"I can't say that I have. I would have remembered her."

"Mr. Hopkins are you only here during the day?"

"Yes, Monday to Friday. I am the only General Manager. We have an evening/night shift supervisor who works from 6 p.m. to 6 a.m.

"Will this supervisor be in this evening?

"As a matter of fact, Calvin is here right now. He is completing education in hotel management. We provide internal education programs to selected employees to further their careers, here at the Windsor Park Hotel. His next shift will be tomorrow evening."

"Then we need to speak with him right now," Ross said.

"Of course, follow me Please. Mr. Hopkins came around from behind his desk and lead them to the back of the hotel, to the "Pavilion Room" where the education was being held. The room was large, but bland, beige walls with table and chairs. Ross thought, this is a room the public doesn't see.

"Please wait here." Mr. Hopkins walked in and whispered something in the educator's ear, walked over to who Ross, assumed was Calvin and both men, walked out. Detectives Shapiro and Ross, this is Calvin Thomas, our Evening Supervisor."

Mr. Thomas was probably younger than twenty-five years old. He was eager, Shapiro noted he was listening to them, while at the same time, listening to the lecturer talk about "conflict resolution."

"Detectives!" Calvin forgot to use his inner voice. "What's this about? I haven't done anything wrong."

"No one said you did, and we need your undivided attention," Shapiro clearly told him.

"Have you seen this young lady at anytime during your shifts? "She would have been around later in the evening." Shapiro showed him the picture of Skylar with the blonde wig.

Ross noticed a shift in the kid's stance as soon as he looked at the picture. He had become anxious, rubbing the back of his neck with his hand. He looked at Mr. Hopkins. He abruptly handed the picture back to Shapiro. Ross got a feeling, the kid knew something, but didn't want to say with his boss standing there.

"Mr. Hopkins, we'll take it from here. Thanks for your help. We would like to question Mr. Thomas privately." Shapiro gave Ross a "what are you doing look," while Mr. Hopkins excused himself.

"Calvin its just us, now spill. I know you know more. This woman was murdered, so if you know something, you need to tell us." Ross said firmly.

"She's dead? She was a classy lady. She would come in late, sit at the bar and order an apple martini. She was beautiful. I can't believe she's dead. Her name was Catherine. She waited at the bar for the same man. He would come and get her, and they would go upstairs to room 1102."

Shapiro showed Calvin a picture of the gentleman and Skylar together, however the gentleman's face could not be seen, only the back of his head. He was hiding from the cameras. "Do you recognize this gentleman? Is he the man that would come downstairs to escort Catherine upstairs?"

Both Ross and Shapiro noticed that Calvin was having a tough time trying to determine if this was the same man. He stared at the photo for a while longer and was shaking his head from side to side.

"I don't know. I never really looked at him, let alone the back of his head. The hair color is the same. He would come down and escort her upstairs. They didn't sit at the bar or talk to anyone downstairs."

"Do you know anything about him, like his name? What he does for a living? Is he here often?"

"I don't know who he is, but I could tell he was really into her. He treated her like a lady. I knew why she was here, but it was none of my business though."

"Is there any way, we could find out who reserved room 1102 on three separate dates, last month?" Ross asked.

Calvin just stared at Ross. This time even Shapiro saw the anxiety creeping up. He was panicking. He didn't want to answer because he was afraid.

"You alright? You're sweating and pale. You look like you're going to pass out. Do you want to sit down? Ross asked.

"No, I'm fine. Mr. Hopkins thinks that we don't know about room 1102. The employees know."

"That's why you didn't want to say anything in front of him. What about room 1102?"

"The hotel does a lot of business with the city and the city does a lot of business internationally, so to accommodate these influential, rich businessmen, a room is always available to them, when needed. Its not just businessmen. lawyers, judges, and politicians have used it. It is reserved, but not in the usual way. Discretion is of the utmost importance. These individuals go directly through Mr. Hopkins. He's never here in the evening when the action happens, so he doesn't have a clue. He's never seen Catherine in the hotel."

"Would Mr. Hopkins know who may have "needed" the room, on a particular night?" Shapiro was curious.

"I don't really know. I don't know anything about how the room is reserved. Look I know you are going to question Mr. Hopkins again. I don't want to lose my job over this.

"Thanks for your help."

Shapiro had a hunch. He went to the front desk and asked if room 1102 could be reserved.

"I'm sorry sir, room 1102 is a private room and can't be reserved. Our reserved rooms don't go any higher than 720," the front desk receptionist explained.

Shapiro played stupid. "Oh, I must have gotten the wrong room number. Thank you. Is Mr. Hopkins available to meet with Detectives Shapiro and Ross?"

"One moment please. I will let him know you wish to see him."

Mr. Hopkins stepped out of his office and gestured for both detectives to come into his office.

"Mr. Hopkins can you tell us about room 1102, seeing as it is a private room and can't be reserved."

The General Manager became quiet and sat down in his executive chair. "How did you find out? I thought I was being so discreet, as Mr. Parker requested."

"Your employees know about room 1102, Mr. Hopkins. Now you want to fill us in," Shapiro said sharply.

"The Parker family owns the Windsor Park Hotel. It has been here for the last eighty years. I have worked here for the last twenty-five years. I started as a bell boy and worked my way up. Sometimes I am asked to look the other way, by my employer. I don't ask questions because it's none of my business."

"What were you asked to do, by your employer?" Shapiro demanded.

"It's nothing illegal, just unethical in my opinion. Suite 1102 is the private residence of the Parker family. It is used when they are in town. They don't live here. They live in Montreal. The suite has everything you would ever want. You can stay for days really, without leaving. The Parkers have many influential friends, who bring in their influential friends and money to the hotel and the city.

Therefore, when one of Mr. Parker's friends requests the room for whatever reason, the request is granted. The request goes through me, so there are no discrepancies. Until now it has been done so discreetly."

"Mr. Hopkins, we don't care about the room. We want to know who was in it for 3 nights last month. There is a photo we would like you to look at. It is the back of a gentleman's head. He is with a young lady. The young lady is the murder victim I spoke to you about when I came in and asked for the footage."

"Of course," Mr. Hopkins looked at the photo and his expression was one of familiarity. "I think this is Judge Theodore Hamilton. He comes in from time to time for a drink with colleagues in late afternoon."

"Are you sure?" Ross wanted him to be sure.

"Yes, I'm fairly certain this is Judge Hamilton."

Ross and Shapiro just gave each other a look "great we need to question a Judge about a high-priced escort. Just wonderful," Shapiro said, while shaking his head.

"Thank you for your help, Mr. Hopkins. I only have one more question, "Shapiro had a feeling."

"Yes, what is it?"

"Do the Parkers also own the Savoy Hotel?"

"They bought the hotel about fifteen years ago. Why do you ask?

"Just a question. Thanks again for your co-operation."

Shapiro and Ross walked out of the hotel and a short distance to the car. "That would explain why the victim had appointments at the Savoy, as well. The same thing was happening there. No doubt, the Parkers have a suite there as well, they were letting their friends use, when needed."

"I'm sure you're right, partner," Shapiro said.

They were silent for a while. Ross was thinking of Jade, as he was looking out the window. It was eleven in the morning; she was probably just getting up and jumping in the shower. He would love to be there with her to lather her up all over, but he knew he had to stay away from her, or he would just keep sleeping with her and she deserved so much better. He wasn't ready to commit. He was confused. He needed to focus on this murder.

"His thoughts were interrupted when he heard Shapiro say, "hey are you listening to me at all? "Where the hell were you? We need to question Judge Hamilton. We better have all our i's dotted and t's crossed."

"Let's go for lunch and while we're there, we can call his office. Maybe, he can see us today." Ross said.

"Sounds good. I need to look at the footage from the Savoy. Maybe there could be another player. She had three appointments there last month, as well."

CHAPTER 10

JADE HAD FINALLY MADE IT out of bed around ten-thirty. She was sore all over, but it was a wonderful sore. That man knew how to please a woman. She threw herself in the shower and let the fairly hot water just fall on her sore muscles. She used every muscle having sex with Mark, yesterday afternoon, then twice more after supper. She finally fell asleep around eleven-thirty last night.

Today, she was going to concentrate on her sister's Celebration of Life. She wanted Kim to help her. She needed to call Kim first. Jade didn't know if she was working or not.

"Hey Kim, its Jade, how are you doing?"

"Hey Jade, I was going to call you today. I was wondering how you're doing. I'm good."

"Are you working today? If not, I was wondering if we could get together. I would really like your help with Skylar's Celebration of Life. You were her best friend."

Kim's eyes began to water, "I miss her so much. I'm not sleeping well and there are times where I swear, I hear her voice. I would love to help you plan her Celebration of Life. I have a couple of pictures of her being really silly. She was so much fun."

Jade thought, pictures right. I am going to have to drive back home to pick up pictures of Skylar as she was growing up. "She was a lot of fun. I miss her too. I miss everything about her."

"Do you have any ideas of where it can be held, Kim?

"I would like to have her celebration at the hospital, if possible. That's where all her friends were. She loved being a nurse. What do you think Jade?"

"I think having it at the hospital is a wonderful idea. Some of her colleagues were so worried that they wouldn't be able to attend because they would be working. This way, depending on the time it is scheduled for, they can all attend."

"We can discuss an appropriate time that will be accommodating to her friends and colleagues, when we get together. How does that sound?" Jade said

"Sounds good. Where do you want to meet?"

"Do you want to come to the hotel? We can have a late lunch on me."

"Be there in a half hour Jade."

"Sounds good."

Kim and Jade discussed the details of the celebration. Kim had called her supervisor, Ms. Lasalle about booking a room for it. They discussed a come and go with finger foods and non alcohol beverages. They decided having it from 6 p.m. to 8 p.m., would cover both shifts for colleagues to attend.

"I have to drive back to the Sault tomorrow to pick up some pictures of Skylar. I'll be back the following day. Please let me know when the room is booked. Next week would be perfect. We can let people know by word of mouth. What do you think Kim? I don't want to announce it in the obituary. I want her closest friends to attend, not just people that knew her."

"I think that's fine. I can post it on our hospital board at work. Maybe put up an announcement with a beautiful picture of Skylar."

"That sounds wonderful. Thanks for your help, Kim. I couldn't have done this without out you. You were a loyal friend to her. She loved you."

"I would have done just about anything for her."

"Kim, you knew about Skylar being an escort, didn't you?"

Kim just looked at Jade. "I did. She made me promise not to say anything to anyone. Skylar was a free spirit. She had the best spirit of anyone I know."

"Kim, why didn't she tell me? Why didn't she confide in me?"

"Are you kidding me, telling you would have been like telling her mother. She was afraid you wouldn't understand. She thought you would have been disappointed in her. Skylar didn't want to hurt you, Jade. She always said that you and her were very different. She wanted to experience

85

different things. Being an escort was something that most people thought was disrespectful and associated with such a negative stigma, but Skylar didn't."

"I don't know how I would have reacted if she had told me." Jade admitted.

"Most people think that being an escort is all about sex. Skylar told me the majority of her clients didn't care about sex, as much as conversation and general intimacy. Its surprised me to learn, that sex wasn't actually a big part of being an escort. Skylar admitted this." She was making the money she wanted to make and having a good time doing it. She was happy, Jade. She loved you more than anything. She would have done anything for you. Skylar always talked about her big sister."

"I'm glad she had you to confide in and thank you for being honest Kim."

Just before leaving the hotel, Kim received a phone call from Ms. Lasalle.

"Hello Kim, just to let you know the Superior meeting room has been booked for next Monday for the celebration."

"That's great Amanda. Thank you. I'll let Jade know." Kim hung up.

"We got a room Jade!" Kim said.

Jade needed to drive back home to pick up pictures and more clothes. While home she wanted to touch base with the Longos. She was going to let Mark know what she was doing. She called his cell phone, however he didn't pick up, so she left a message.

"Hey Mark, its Jade. I just wanted to let you know that I'm driving to the Sault right now. I spoke with Kim about Skylar's Celebration of Life. It will be next Monday night at the hospital. I need to pick up pictures and other things and should be back the day after tomorrow. Call me later."

CHAPTER 11

ROSS AND SHAPIRO WERE SITTING at their desks, going over footage from the Savoy Hotel. Ross heard his cell phone ringing, picked it up and looked at the caller I.D. He muted the phone and put it back down.

"Must have not been important,' Shapiro said.

"I'll deal with it later. I just want to focus on the footage. We need a break in this case."

"I agree with you." Shapiro said with frustration.

Shapiro's cell phone rang. Caller ID showed an unknown caller. Shapiro answered the call.

"That's great, we'll be there at four p.m. Thanks."

Shapiro turned to Ross, "that was the courthouse, Judge Hamilton will see us at four p.m. Keep looking at the footage, I'm going to the little boy's room."

Ross took the opportunity to listen to his messages. He knew Jade had called. He was curious as to whether she had left a message. She did, but he knew he wasn't going to call her. He knew he was being an ass, who was going to hurt her. A little hurt now is better than a lot of pain later. The timing was awful.

Ross and Shapiro entered the courthouse on Elm Street and took the stairs up to the second floor. Judge Hamilton's chambers were at the end of the hallway. Ross and Shapiro introduced themselves and they were asked to have a sit.

"He will be with you in a few minutes." The male assistant said. The waiting area was elegantly decorated in variations of rich browns. Pictures of the courthouse from decades ago hung on the walls.

"Judge Hamilton will see you now. The male assistant escorted them in."

Ross and Shapiro entered the Judge's chambers. The walls were a taupe color, with mahogany wainscoting and a desk made of the same rich wood. The sweet smell of the wood was unmistakable. The room had so much character. The rustic brown leather chairs were inviting. Behind the desk were shelves of law books. On his desk, the Judge had a framed photo of himself with his family. His children were grown. There were framed photos of his children with his grandchildren.

Judge Theodore Hamilton himself was a tall man, who wore expensive suits with confidence. He had piercing hazel eyes and was handsome for a sixty-four-year-old. He had salt and pepper hair that remained thick and a moustache to match. When he spoke, he was articulate and didn't mince his words. He had a no-nonsense type of character.

"Detectives, please take a seat and tell me why you asked for this meeting."

"Judge Hamilton we are investigating the murder of Skylar Rose."

"I don't know anyone by that name."

"You wouldn't have known her as Skylar Rose, but rather Catherine. She was an escort."

While Shapiro was questioning the Judge, Ross was looking for any variation in body language or shift that would tell him, they hit a nerve. Ross noticed the Judge stiffened and avoided eye contact for a second, when he heard the name "Catherine."

Shapiro took out the picture of the Judge and Catherine. "This is a picture of Skylar Rose as Catherine. The gentleman she is with, although only the back of his head is visible, is believed to be you."

Shapiro was looking directly at the Judge when he asked, "Is this you Judge Hamilton?"

Judge Hamilton took the picture and looked at it for a fair bit of time. He looked at it with such fondness. "Your telling me the murdered young lady the news reported about, was Catherine?"

"So, you do know her." Ross asked.

"Yes, I know her. Knew her. We would meet a couple of times per month at the Windsor Park Hotel. We would be together for two or three hours. The conversation was stimulating. She was lovely. I enjoyed spending time with her. She was intelligent and quite versed in many topics of conversation. She was captivating. I can't believe she's gone."

"How did you meet her or make contact with her?" Shapiro asked.

"A very good friend of mine, Jean-Luc Gervais, who lives in Paris and is a highly successful restaurateur, gave me her phone number. Jean-Luc would see her when he came to Canada. She would meet with him in Toronto. He hasn't been to Canada for four months now.

"Before you ask, I haven't been in the country for the last couple of weeks. My entire family along with invited guests, have been in the Dominican. My youngest daughter just got married there last week. We arrived back in Canada three days ago. I can have my assistant email the entire itinerary, including hotel accommodations and anything else you may need."

"Judge Hamilton, thank you for your cooperation. We will be confirming your story."

"Gentlemen, one last thing, I am asking for and expecting the utmost discretion in this matter. I have been forthright with you, as I have nothing to hide, and I want the murder of this young lady solved. However, I do have myself and family to think about. If you intend to drag my name through the mud, rest assured that I will take action against you, Sudbury Police Services, and the Chief of Police. The mayor is a close friend."

Shapiro reassured the Judge they were not on a witch hunt. They wanted justice for the murder victim. "Judge Hamilton, we want what you want for this woman. Our objective is not to hurt anyone. I am curious, however," Shapiro said.

"You're wondering why I would see an escort from time to time, when I have a beautiful wife at home. My wife is a wonderful woman. She's a great mother, grandmother, friend, and socialite, but she forgot how to be a great wife, somewhere along the way. I enjoyed Catherine's company and I'm not talking about sex. There was very little of that, believe it or not. I had conflicts and she would help me through them. We laughed together and at times cried together. I'm truly going to miss her. She was a confidante."

Both Shapiro and Ross left the Judge with his own thoughts and walked out of the courthouse to Shapiro's car.

"The Judge appeared to be heartbroken. There was nothing out of the ordinary about his body language. He could have kicked us out of his chambers with our tails between our legs, but he didn't. I'll check out his story, but he appeared to be genuine and sincere. I also think on some level and in his own way, he loved "Catherine," Shapiro said.

"I got the same impression," Ross said.

CHAPTER 12

JADE WAS BACK IN SAULT Ste. Marie. It was just after supper time. She ate very little. She just wasn't hungry. Before she left Sudbury, she called Mr. Barnes and asked if it would be possible to pick up her sister's ashes. She explained, she was going back home for a few days and wouldn't be bringing her sister's ashes to the Celebration of Life planned for next week. It would be too sad, and she wanted people to remember Skylar the way she was. After all, this is what Skylar always wanted.

Walking into her apartment, she felt empty. Although, she was here with her sister's ashes, for some reason she felt closer to Skylar in Sudbury. She thought, I'm never going to dial her phone number' speak to her again or text her. She began to sob, holding the urn.

A little while later, she composed herself and placed the urn on the fireplace mantel, close to a photo of her and Skylar. She went to her bedroom and took out some old photo albums from the storage ottoman at the end of her bed. She carried them to the kitchen table and began looking through them. Jade found photos of Skylar as a baby, of them together holding hands when they were seven or eight years old, and Skylar in her soccer uniform when she was in high school. There were birthday pictures at various ages, Christmas photos with their parents, grand-parents, and graduations. Jade thought, Skylar was so beautiful. She had tears in her eyes, lightly rubbing her thumb over her sister's face, and when she blinked, a single tear dropped. She was all alone now.

It was later in the evening, Jade moved to the couch with photos of Skylar. She was so tired, she fell asleep on the couch, with her sister's photos in her hands.

Jade woke up the next morning with a kink in her neck and photos of Skylar in her hands. She got up looking for her phone and found it under a pile of photos on the coffee table. She was so tired last night; she was out like a light. She thought she had missed Mark's call and because she didn't call him back, he would worry. She would call him but when looking at her phone, she found no message from him or missed call.

"I'm sure he got my message yesterday," she said to herself. Why is he not calling me back? Is he avoiding me? Jade asked herself. Its just been one day. He's probably busy, but his phone is always with him. Jade thought, this is one of those times, she would call her sister for advice but that won't be possible. She was going to have to figure things out herself. She knew she wouldn't be calling Mark again. Ball was now in his court. Let's see what he does with it, Jade thought.

Jade took a couple of hours to choose the photos that she wanted to use at the celebration. She put them in a manilla envelope and placed them in her travelling bag. She wanted to go to the restaurant and speak to the Longos before she left for Sudbury, tomorrow morning. She watered her plants, packed more clothes, and jumped into the shower.

Jade arrived at the restaurant just in time for lunch. She was hungry. She hadn't eaten much yesterday. She walked in and could hear the tranquil sounds of water flowing from the fountain located in the middle of the restaurant and filled with coins at the bottom. Coins would be thrown into the fountain as patrons made wishes. It was a beautiful restaurant with stocked wine cabinets and assorted liquor bottles. The tables were covered with vinyl burgundy table covers. It made it easier to clean. Chairs were black vinyl for the same reason. The lighting was dim as the fountain lit up the main dining room. In the centre of the room was a beautiful chandelier that sparkled against the water.

"Jade your back," Domenica Longo said. The older Italian woman came to her with open arms. "Its so good to see you. Are you back for good, sweetheart?"

"Unfortunately, not Mrs. Longo. I came home to get photos of Skylar. I am planning a Celebration of Life for her. Her best friend is helping me. It will be held this Monday coming up, at the hospital where she worked. I needed the photos for a picture board. I also needed more clothes."

"I can't tell you how sorry my husband and I are for your loss, my dear. If there is anything we can do, please let us know. How are you holding up?" Mrs. Longo asked.

"I will not be able to return to work right now. After the celebration, I need to deal with my sister's affairs. I don't even know where to start. I think about having to go through her personal affects and I just want to cry. I'm holding it together for now." Jade explained.

"When my sister Angela died, I had such a grim time going through things, but at least I had the rest of my family. My siblings, which made it easier. We reminisced about her, remembering what a fabulous cook she was, her laughter, and the way she wouldn't let any of us get away with anything. We got in to so much trouble. We laughed and cried. I can't imagine what you are going through. You take all the time you need Bella Mia."

"Thank you, Mrs. Longo. Is Mr. Longo here? I would like to say hello before I leave."

"No, my dear. He is at an appointment with one of our suppliers."

"That's too bad. Please say hello for me. I will be back as soon as I have everything organized. Thank you once again for your understanding. I will be in touch."

"Jade you can't leave without eating. Come, sit down with me. We will have spaghetti and meatballs, with home made bread. You need to eat. You look like you've lost weight Bella. You won't be any good to anyone if you end up in the hospital."

Jade thought, oh I know exactly what you mean. "Sure, I would love that, thank you. I haven't had a plate of spaghetti and meatballs since I left here."

They ate and talked. Jade thought, she needed that plate of pasta. It hit the spot. She needed to see familiar faces. During their meal, co-workers took the time to give their condolences to Jade. She didn't really associate with any of her co-workers, outside of work. This was more her fault. She was older than the twenty-year old's that worked there and felt she would have nothing in common with them. Jade was more the introvert, as opposed to Skylar. Skylar was the life of the party.

It was almost three p.m. by the time she left the restaurant. She had given Mrs. Longo a big hug and told her she would be back soon. She was looking around, while stopped at a red light. She thought to herself, why do I feel so lost here? There is absolutely nothing here for me, except for my job and the Longos. Most of my friends have moved away to bigger cities for their careers and the few I do have here, have families of their own. Why didn't I move to Sudbury when Skylar asked me to?

When she heard car horns blaring, it shook her out of her thoughts. Apparently, the light was green, and she wasn't moving. She accelerated, and the horns stopped.

Once home, she asked herself the same question "why didn't she move to Sudbury?" The city was much bigger than the Sault. There were more restaurants where she could work and there was more to do. The Sault was quaint and homey. It was familiar."

Jade and Skylar were born and raised in the Sault. They went to elementary school and high school here. Their parents were buried here. She thought, the Sault is all I know, but Skylar wanted more. Jade couldn't blame her. Jade always played it safe. She wasn't as trusting as Skylar. She said to herself, "I want to do more with my life. I need something different."

Jade spent the rest of the day cleaning her apartment, watering the rest of her plants, doing laundry, and packing to leave the next morning. She still hadn't heard from Mark. He's clearly sending a message, she thought. One of, sorry but I'm not interested, but thanks for the great sex three times over. Jade's eyes started watering. She should have known better.

Shapiro walked into the station and saw Ross just sitting there, looking straight ahead. He looked lost. "What are you thinking about?"

"Nothing, the case is all."

"You're full of shit. We've known each other for a long time. You've never had that look about any case we've worked on. Don't insult my intelligence, Mark. You keep forgetting I'm older than you and have been married for a long time. Do you want to talk about it?"

"No, lets solve this murder."

"If you need to talk, I'm here, just remember that."

Shapiro sat down at his desk and looked at a folder with Judge Hamilton's name on it. It contained his itinerary for his time away in the Dominican for his daughter's wedding. It also contained a guest list. The list was not short of influential people, like fellow judges, lawyers, and the mayor.

"It contained signed receipts for a week of golf, during the time our victim was killed. I checked with the Airline and the Judge was on their manifest. His passport was swiped for departure to the Dominican on June 17 and swiped again for return to Canada July 2. His daughter got married in Punta Cana at the Eden Roc Cap Cana on June 22. There are signed receipts by the Judge for room service. The rest of the time was a vacation for the family and friends. His alibi was solid."

"Another dead end. What about the footage from the Savoy Hotel? We did see the victim with another gentleman. We need to find out who he is. Let's go pay Marcus Cruz a visit."

The ride to the Savoy Hotel on the Kingsway, was a quiet one. Shapiro knew Ross was thinking of Jade. Normally, Ross was the talker in the car. He would talk about sports, work, city events, taxes and whatever else came to mind. Today he was silent. Shapiro wanted to help his partner but didn't want to intrude or overstep his boundaries.

They arrived at the hotel, parked, and walked into the beautiful lobby. The lobby of this hotel was smaller than the Windsor Park. It had all the charm and elegance of an historical landmark. The hotel was decorated in warm earthy tones of browns, pale oranges, and pale yellows. It had more wood than the Windsor Park. The front desk was made of a brilliant cherry wood that glistened. Looking at it, it was full of character. It was curved in some areas with beautiful ornate designs carved into it. The floors were a light beige marble. Photos of the city from different years decorated the walls. There were fewer windows and plenty of plants. Two chandeliers lit up the lobby.

Ross went to the front desk and asked the receptionist if Mr. Cruz was available. He introduced himself and showed his badge.

"One moment please, I will check for you," the receptionist said.

'Thank you."

Mr. Cruz came out of the back room and extended his hand to both Ross and Shapiro. He was of Hispanic decent, average height, meticulous dresser, and was all about customer service. "Detectives how can I be of service to you? I hope the footage that I sent to you was helpful."

"The footage was helpful; however, we are having a tough time identifying a gentleman. He would have been here closer to eleven p.m., two nights last month. I am assuming that as the General Manager you work during the day. Is that correct?"

"I enjoy working during the day, but I also work during the evening. I like to know who comes into the hotel during the evening. Perhaps, I can look at the photo of the gentleman you are inquiring about. I may have seen him or know him."

"Ross showed him the photo of the gentleman with Skylar, also known as Catherine. I know this gentleman. Mr. Cruz was surprised. His name is Ryder Campbell. He is one of the richest Real Estate Developers in the country. The woman with him looks familiar but I can't recall where I've seen her. She is beautiful. It figures a man like that with a woman like her."

"Does he stay here often?" Shapiro asked.

"Two to three times a month. He builds condominiums, but he also builds malls and hotels. He has influential friends in Sudbury. One being the mayor"

"Is he good friends with the Parkers? Does he always stay in the same room and if so, what room is it?

Ross noticed a shift in Mr. Cruz's stance. The big smile he had on his face, dimmed a little. He didn't appear as if he wanted to help as much.

"Mr. Cruz, please answer my question. We know the Parkers have a room they use at the Windsor Park, when they are in town and let close friends use when needed. I'm sure they have one here. Am I right?"

"You're right, Detective Ross. Mr. Parker tells me when they or one of their guests will be arriving to use the room. I ensure they are given the special treatment. It's none of my concern what goes on in that room. I have no control over that."

"Would you have Mr. Campbell's contact information. We need to speak with him?"

"What a coincidence because he will be here tomorrow."

Mr. Cruz gave Ross the information he requested and excused himself. "Gentlemen if there is nothing else, I really should be getting back to my work."

"Thank you for your cooperation. If there is anything else, we'll be in touch."

Shapiro and Ross left their cards with Mr. Cruz. They walked out of the hotel and to the car. Shapiro immediately called Ryder Campbell.

"Mr. Campbell, this is Detective Shapiro with the Sudbury Police Services. I am investigating the homicide of Skylar Rose and I need your assistance."

"Detective Ross, I have no idea what you're talking about, and I certainly don't know anyone by the name of Skylar Rose. What is this about? I will be in Sudbury tomorrow morning and will be staying at the Savoy Hotel. I can meet you in the restaurant of the hotel, say around ten a.m., but I only have an hour, as I have a meeting with your mayor at eleven a.m."

"Both my partner and I will meet you at ten a.m. tomorrow morning."

Mr. Campbell just hung up. "Busy guy, Shapiro thought.

It was mid afternoon and both Shapiro and Ross were working on paperwork. They were also going over notes in their little black notebooks. "The only common denominator here is "The Parkers" and that's because they own both the hotels the victim had her "appointments," otherwise there is nothing." Shapiro said.

"There has to be another connection. We just don't have all the pieces of the puzzle, is all." Ross added.

"Shapiro was thinking out loud, "we need to complete a thorough background check on both Judge Hamilton and Ryder Campbell. I want to know everything about them. Maybe there's something in their backgrounds that may lead to a connection. Right now, all we have is these two persons of interest."

It was after six p.m. by the time they finished their paperwork. Shapiro was going to start the background checks tomorrow. He wanted to go home to his wife right now.

"So, what are you doing tonight?"

Ross was just about to answer when his phone rang. He identified himself, "Detective Ross."

"Detective Ross, this is Calvin from the Windsor Park Hotel. I forgot to tell you something the other day when you and your partner were here. It slipped my mind, until I went outside tonight."

"What would that be?"

"When Catherine was ready to leave the hotel, she would request a cab. I would always escort her out to the front of the hotel where they were parked, waiting for hotel guests. There was always a dark sedan, maybe a Mercedes or BMW, parked across the street. The color was black, or dark blue. Windows were tinted dark and as soon as the cab drove away, the sedan would make a "U" turn and leave as well. It almost seemed like the sedan was following the cab. I've never seen the sedan again."

"Did you by any chance get a look at the driver or a licence plate number?"

"No, I'm sorry. It was too dark outside."

"Thanks for the information."

Ross let Shapiro know what the phone call was about before he went home. "Just another piece of the puzzle."

Ross was on his way home when he drove by the Holiday Inn. He noticed Jade's car was in the parking area. She was back, he thought. He wanted to see her. He hadn't known her for a long time, but there was something special about her. He felt it the minute he laid his eyes on her. He couldn't stop thinking about her. He had made it home and was still thinking of Jade. He thought about how soft she was, and how beautiful she looked when they were having sex. She called his name in such a satisfied way, it just made him want to please her more. He was getting hard just thinking of her.

"This is crazy, he said to himself. What the hell is wrong with me? Why am I so afraid of getting close to this woman? I keep telling myself she lives out of town, and this is going to go nowhere. I don't want to hurt her. Well, she's a big girl though. She can handle it. Maybe, she's not looking for anything meaningful." He kept saying that to himself, hoping that he would eventually believe it, but no such luck. He went to bed, with thoughts of Jade on his mind, and one major hard on.

CHAPTER 13

THE NEXT MORNING, ROSS AND Shapiro decided to show up early for their meeting with Ryder Campbell. "You look tired my friend. Not sleeping well. Thoughts keeping you awake?" Shapiro knew he was being a bit of a shit.

Ross felt like he got run over by a freight train. He tossed and turned all night. "I don't want to talk about it," he said.

They entered the restaurant, when a gentleman who looked like a preppy nerd, holding a computer, and carrying a man purse, asked, "are you Detectives Ross and Shapiro?"

"Yes, who are you?"

He walked out of the restaurant, without answering their question. A few seconds later he reappeared with who Ross and Shapiro, assumed was Ryder Campbell.

Mr. Campbell was younger than what Shapiro originally thought, maybe mid thirties. I'm sure the ladies found him extremely attractive, with his blue eyes and blonde shaggy hair. He was tanned and looked like the all-American California surfer. He was tall and fit and wore his expensive Armani suits well.

"Gentlemen, I'm sorry about sending Patrick in first. I wanted to make sure I was speaking to the right people. I don't like to waste my time. Patrick will join us in case I need him and to take notes. Would you like breakfast?"

"No thank you, we'll just have coffee. We are investigating the murder of Skylar Rose."

"I have already told you, I don't' know this person."

Ross took the photo of Ryder and Catherine out of his jacket pocket and asked, "do you know this woman?"

"Yes, I know this woman. Her name is Catherine. She and I would spend time together while I was here on business. Is this Skylar Rose? Is this the murder victim, I keep hearing about on the news?"

"Who would want to hurt her. She was wonderful, just lovely."

"When was the last time you saw her?

The assistant, Patrick was tapping keys on the computer and when he was done, he turned the computer around to face Ryder. It was a calendar which indicated the last time he was in town.

"According to my scheduler, the last time would have been June 24 at ten-thirty p.m. We went upstairs and she left around two in the morning. I walked her out, hailed her a cab and she left. That was the last time I saw her. I received an emergency phone call the next morning and left for Victoria, British Columbia."

"Where were you between June 27 and June 30."

"Patrick, that's fine, he said when he noticed his assistant was tapping away. I know exactly where I was. The emergency phone call I received was from my sister Allison. She called to tell me, our father was dying, and I was needed home. He died two days later in hospital. Complications of Congestive Heart Failure and Chronic Obstructive Pulmonary Disease. My father loved his cigarettes and cigars. Both my sister and I needed to make funeral arrangements. My father didn't believe in pre-planning funeral arrangements."

Ross gave his condolences and could see that Mr. Campbell was having a tough time speaking about his father. He was trying to keep it together.

"I stayed at the Hotel Fairmont Empress in Victoria. My father's wake was on June 27 and the funeral was the next day. I flew back to Toronto June 30. I needed to get back to work. Your mind wonders with too much time off. I will have Patrick email you all the necessary documentation you need. Also, I will call Flynn's Funeral Home and give them permission to speak with you. Patrick will give you my sister's contact information, both home and cell phone."

"Mr. Campbell when you escorted Catherine out of the hotel to hail a cab, did you see a black sedan around at all? Ross was curious.

"No, I can't say that I did. Honestly, I wasn't looking for one. I just wanted to make sure Catherine got a cab."

One last question, Mr. Campbell. "How did you meet Catherine?"

"I am never in one city for more than two weeks, sometimes less. I met her at the Royal York Hotel in Toronto about five months ago. I had business meetings with Australian developers one evening and she was sitting at the bar, sipping on a martini. She was gorgeous, tall, shapely, and so confident. That's what attracted me to her. I was experienced enough to know why she was there. Being the confident man, I am, I introduced myself, gave her my card and told her to call me. She told me she didn't live in Toronto. I told her it didn't matter; I would meet her anywhere. She called about a month later and we met at the Savoy Hotel in Sudbury. I have been seeing her ever since. This would happen two to three times per month. She typically would spend a couple of hours with her clients. She spent the whole night with me, the first time. Money was not an issue. She was not only sexy as all hell, but highly intelligent. I enjoyed our conversations. She was the whole package, beautiful and smart.

"Thank you for your time, Mr. Campbell. We'll be in touch if we have any further questions. Ross gave him his card. We will be expecting all the documentation we spoke about. We need to check out your story."

"Of course, gentleman."

All three men shook hands and Ross, and Shapiro left the restaurant. "So, what do you think? Anything you noticed about body language?"

"No, nothing. That is one confident man, and I think he is telling the truth. These men thought the world of Catherine."

Ross thought, if she is anything like her sister, I can understand why.

Ryder Campbell made arrangement to move his eleven-a.m. meeting with the mayor to one p.m. He gave Patrick the time off until then. He was shaken to hear about Catherine.

He returned to his room that was elegantly decorated and full of character, like the rest of the hotel. He sat down at the sandalwood desk and thought about his last encounter with Catherine. She was wearing a little black dress; black stilettos and her blonde hair was up loosely. He couldn't wait to kiss the nape of her neck and that's where he began. He kissed her neck, then her lips, and back to her neck, while unzipping her dress. He helped her out of the dress. Her lingerie was enough to bring a man to his knees. That night she had on a laced teddy in a red color. They enjoyed and explored each other. Her mouth was soft and sensual. She satisfied him like no other. He very much enjoyed her company.

He remembered looking at her after their last encounter, "I know your going to leave now but I want you to stay. I don't care how much it costs me. Please stay." He asked.

Catherine did stay and they had a wonderful night together. Catherine was easy to be with.

Ryder was thinking so intently about his last encounter with Catherine, he didn't realize he had a hard on. He was going to take a shower and while in there, take care of his hard on.

Jade was out purchasing a few items for the Celebration of Life. She lost track of time; it was almost three p.m. She and Kim were going to meet this weekend to put everything together for Monday evening. Kim was responsible for the food and beverages, and she was responsible for the picture boards and decorations. Skylar loved, lavender colored flowers. Jade ordered two "Peace and Hope" lavender bouquets and two "Gracious Lavender" baskets. She would pick them up on Monday. She was going to put the pictures into frames that would hold multiple pictures. She thought, three frames would do it, with single pictures of her. Jade needed to write a little blurb for each picture. This was going to take the entire weekend.

Her thoughts were interrupted when her phone started to ring. "Hello."

"Hey Jade, its Kim! I was wondering, do you want to stay at my place for the weekend? We can help each other out.

"Sure, that sounds good."

"Great, come on over anytime. I took time off to get things ready. I'm off until Tuesday."

"How about tomorrow around supper? I'll bring Chinese food." Jade said.

"Terrific, see you tomorrow." Kim hung up before Jade could say anything further.

I can't believe there's going to be a Celebration of Life for that tramp. She doesn't deserve any kind of celebration. She had everybody fooled. If people only knew the real, her. All she was good at was having sex for money and screwing people around. A true slut. She only cared about herself. No one else was important. It didn't matter who she stomped on. That's fine. I made sure she wasn't going to be with anyone, especially "him."

CHAPTER 14

JADE WAS JUST STEPPING OUT of the shower when she heard her cell phone ringing. She would dry off first and check for messages once she was done. She didn't think it would be Mark. He made it clear she was only a one-night stand. If it were him, he could wait till she was good and ready to call, if she called at all.

She finished getting ready and checked her messages. It was Kim. "Jade I'm going out for a bit. If you come over, the key is under the rock, in the garden. It's the only rock in the garden."

Jade wasn't ready to go over just yet. She needed to pack a few things. Then she needed to purchase the frames.

Getting around this city was harder than the Sault. Sudbury was busy. There was much more traffic. Its funny she thought, how three, four hours of distance could influence culture. The Sault had a large Italian community whereas Sudbury had a large French one.

Jade had finished shopping for the celebration around three p.m. She picked up beautiful frames for the celebration, that she intended to hang in her apartment once she returned home. She brought the frames to her car and the returned to the mall. She didn't plan on it, but she wanted to buy a new dress for her sister's Celebration of Life. She remembered; a beautiful dress that caught her eye, while shopping earlier. She went back to the store and picked out her size. She tried it on and came out of the change room to look at herself in the mirror on the change room door. The dress was beautiful. It was simple but elegant. It was a wine-colored lace, short sleeve, A- line cocktail dress with a V-neck. It had a high waist and was knee length. She liked the way it flowed when she moved in it. She had a pair of black ankle strapped stiletto pumps that would look wonderful with this dress.

"I'll take this dress please."

"You look lovely in it my dear. The way it moves on you is very becoming," the saleswoman said.

"Thank you very much."

Jade paid for the dress and went to her car. She made sure she had everything she would need for this weekend and the celebration. She had the photos in her car. She had a pair of black stiletto pumps back at the hotel. She wanted to bring the dress back to the hotel, rather than keeping it in the bag all weekend, in her car. She would get dressed at the hotel on Monday.

She headed back to the hotel and dropped off the dress. Now, she needed to pick up Chinese food and head over to Kim's.

Jade made it to Kim's place around five-thirty p.m.

"Thanks for staying over this weekend Jade. I can't seem to get my shit together. I'm trying to stay positive but just want to cry. I can't imagine what you're going through."

"I'm holding my own. I take solace in knowing my sister had good friends and she was happy. She was doing what she wanted to do. I just wished we talked more than we did, that's all."

"She loved you Jade, don't doubt that."

"I know. I'm just sad because I didn't really know her the way I thought I did."

They had finished the Chinese food. "Listen why don't you get into something comfortable and wash up, I'll wash these few dishes, then we'll go and sit outside or watch a movie and have a glass of wine. Whatever you want." Kim said.

"Sounds good. I'm going to wash my face, put my hair up in a ponytail and put on lounging pants with a tee shirt."

Jade went into the guest bedroom and retrieved her lounging pants and navy-blue tee shirt. She couldn't wait to take her bra and socks off. Stupid boulder holders, she thought. She changed and went into the bathroom. She cleaned her face, applied moisturizer, brushed her teeth, and put her back in a pony tail. Then, she came out to find, Detective Ross standing in the kitchen. She didn't hear him come in. He must have come in when the water was running, while brushing her teeth.

They both looked directly at each other for what seemed a long time.

"Hello Jade."

"What are you doing here detective?"

"Kim explained, Detective Ross was here to ask her a few more questions."

Jade turned away from Mark, poured herself a glass of wine and stepped outside on the deck, closing the door behind her. She made herself comfortable in one of the Adirondack chairs. She had nothing to say to him.

"Detective Ross, what is it that you wanted to ask me?"

Mark was just staring at Jade. "Sorry, Ms. Marshall. Did Skylar ever mention anything to you about being followed by a dark sedan after her appointments? Primarily from the Windsor Park Hotel."

"No, she didn't mention anything about a dark sedan, but she did tell me once or twice that she had a feeling that she was being watched or followed."

"Did she ever mention who it might be?"

"No, never. It didn't really frighten her though. She went on with life as usual."

"Thank you for your assistance. Have a good evening."

Kim had walked over to the sink and had her back to Detective Ross. She didn't see him, staring at Jade. He turned away and left.

Kim went to the front door and made sure it was locked before she went out back to join Jade. "It's nice outside tonight. The stars are pretty and there's little wind. Do you need a refill?

"No, the wine is good, thanks. Did the detective leave?"

"Yeah, he had a few more questions, so I answered them. No big deal. I noticed you were cold towards him. Is everything okay? That man is easy on the eyes."

"I just didn't feel like talking to him, that's all."

"Jade, I know when someone has it bad for someone else, and you got it bad for him. News flash, he's got it bad for you to. He just doesn't know it yet. Cut him some slack."

Jade just continued to drink her wine. She did have it bad for him. She didn't know what to do. She knew she wouldn't go to him. He made her feel used and that made her feel dirty. He hurt her. She didn't need that in her life.

"Jade did you hear me."

"Yeah, I did. We'll see what happens Kim. I'm going to cook an Italian meal tomorrow night for dinner. That okay with you?" Jade had already picked up all the ingredients she needed for the dinner.

"Oh, for sure, that sounds great Jade. By the way, great way to change the subject."

They sat outside, drinking wine, until they went to bed. Jade thought about Mark. What the hell was his problem? Whatever…. she had to get some sleep. There was lots to do this weekend.

Ross didn't expect to see Jade tonight. It came as a total shock. She was either really angry with him or hated him.

That was evident by the way she was giving him the cold shoulder. He deserved it. He hated himself. He had never seen her with her hair up in a ponytail. Her neck was tantalizing. He could see from her tee shirt; she wasn't wearing a bra; her nipples were hard. Even with lounging pants, a tee shirt on and barefoot, she still looked sexy as hell.

Kim loved the spaghetti and meatballs. She had a second helping. "Kim, I don't know how you stay so tiny, the way you eat. You must have a hollow leg, where you store everything," Jade said.

They spent the weekend putting everything together for Skylar's Celebration of Life. They laughed till their bellies hurt and they cried together, as well.

Jade could understand why Skylar loved Kim so much as a friend. She was funny, kind, direct, loyal, and smarter than what Jade gave her credit for. Down deep Jade was jealous of Kim. Probably because Kim got to spend so much time with Skylar rather than her. Jade realized a couple of things about herself this weekend. The biggest was that she can be so critical of others in her own way. She was so narrow minded. Her expectations were always high. Perhaps, that's why Skylar didn't tell her about being an escort. She didn't want to be judged and hear a long lecture about how she was disrespecting herself. She told Kim because she knew Kim wouldn't give her a big lecture or judge her. Kim accepted Skylar for who she was and the way she was. Jade would have loved a friend like that, but she could never trust anyone enough to have a friend like that.

Jade was just staring at Kim while she was rambling on about this guy, "am I talking to much? Just tell me."

"No, you're funny. I can see why Skylar thought the world of you. You were… still are a good friend to her."

"Skylar was my best friend. Know one will ever be able to hold a candle to her. I know I'll never meet a friend like her anywhere. I want this celebration to be special for her. She loved life and lived it to the fullest. Maybe, she made mistakes along the way, but none of us are perfect."

"You're right Kim, there will never be anyone like her. Thank you for helping me put this all together, I couldn't have done it without you. Your trays look beautiful, a lot of finger foods that Skylar loved. There were dessert, cheese and crackers and fruit trays. She loved graham crackers with cream cheese and strawberry jam. She'd say, "put them together and they taste exactly like a piece of strawberry cheesecake." I also, bought jellybeans and put them into little clear bags. Everyone knew she loved them. She always had them at work."

"Thanks Jade. Thank you for asking me to be a part of this. It makes me feel closer to her. Would you mind if I kept one or two of her baby pictures? I have pictures of her and I from when we first met up till now, but I don't have any of her as a baby."

"Sure, that's no problem. Skylar was a busy baby. I remember my mother telling me, when she was about three, three and a half, she had her days and nights all mixed up. She would sleep during the day, get up during the night, and make her way to the cupboard where the pots and pans were stored, when everyone was sleeping. She would bang on those pots and pans with a large spoon and wake up the house. Mom and dad had to keep her awake during the day for a couple of days to get her system back on track, so she would sleep at night. Even then she was a free spirit."

"You can tell from the photos, she was happy. You did a wonderful job capturing that, Jade. Hey Jade stay over tonight! Go back tomorrow morning. We're done everything. We'll order out and drink wine. You'll have enough time to get ready for the celebration. What do you think?"

"Thanks Kim, but I've got to go. I need to get a good night's rest and pick up the flowers in the morning. Get the room ready and get myself ready."

"Have the flower shop deliver them to the hospital in the morning. We can go to the hospital in the afternoon and set up. I noticed there was nothing going on in the Superior Room, prior to the celebration. Then we can leave and get ready for six p.m."

"That actually sounds like a good plan, Jade thought. Where's the wine then?"

CHAPTER 15

Jade was on the phone with the flower shop when Kim got up. "Thank you so much, that will be such a tremendous help to me. So, they will be delivered around one p.m. then? Wonderful thanks again."

"Did you get any sleep at all," Kim asked. "You look wired."

"I just want everything to be perfect."

"Don't worry Jade, it will be."

"Kim, do you need any help with the trays?"

"No, I'm good. Colleagues from the hospital are coming by to help."

"Hey Jade, thanks for the weekend and thanks for staying last night." Kim had tears in her eyes. "For some reason, when your near, I feel closer to her. I know that sounds weird, but that's how I feel. Could we get together every so often, maybe you come here for the weekend, or I can go to the Sault?"

"I would like that. Its not weird Kim, I feel the same way when you're near. She was a big part of both our lives.

She always will be. Listen, I've got to go. See you at the hospital, this afternoon around two p.m., oh and thanks for such a great weekend."

Ross and Shapiro had gone back to the Windsor Park Hotel to speak with the General Manager about the cameras on the outside of the hotel. In particular, the front of the building where the cabs are parked. Mr. Hopkins explained, "the cameras at the front of the building will show guests getting in and out of cabs and guests coming and going from the hotel. Unfortunately, the cameras do not have the reach to record to the opposite side of the street."

Ross was discouraged. Shapiro was frustrated, "why was the black sedan only seen at this hotel? What was it about this hotel? There has to be a connection."

"We need to find the connection." Ross agreed.

They both went back to the station and Ross was going to start the in-depth background check of both Judge Hamilton and Ryder Campbell. While Shapiro was going to verify Ryder Campbell's alibi for the time of the murder.

In the midst of working, Shapiro asked Ross "you going to the celebration tonight?"

"How did you know the Celebration of Life was tonight?"

"Ross, have you lost your mind. You told me that yesterday. What's wrong with you? I'm starting to worry about you. Are you okay?"

"No, I'm not okay. I can't sleep, I can't think, I hate myself for hurting her but don't see any other way."

"Any other way...... what the hell are you talking about?" Shapiro was confused.

"I don't want to start something I can't finish. I live here, she lives there. She's going home as soon as she deals with her sister's estate. You know how it is."

"No, I don't know how it is. I'm getting a pretty clear picture and the picture I'm getting Ross is that your afraid of commitment. You really like this woman and that's what you're afraid of. You don't know for certain where this relationship might go because you won't talk to her."

Ross just stared at Shapiro. He didn't say anything because he was afraid Shapiro could see that he was right.

"I think we should go to the celebration tonight. I want to check out and observe the guests that attend. I think the killer will be there, Ross."

"You're right. Let's get some supper before we go. It starts at six p.m."

Jade got back to the hotel around four p.m. She and Kim had finished decorating the Superior Room at the hospital and it looked wonderful. Now she needed to get ready. She showered and put her wet hair up in a towel. She put on little make-up but made sure her dark rose-colored lipstick made an impact. She didn't know what she was going to do with her hair. She used large curlers and blow dried her hair, took the curlers out and let her hair fall. She put it up in a messy bun and let strands fall near her face. Bella crystal pierced earrings finished the look. Skylar would love this look, she thought. She needed to leave. She didn't want to drive tonight. Her nerves were frazzled, so she called a cab.

The Superior room at the hospital was decorated with lavender, pink, white, and darker rose-colored flowers that were beautiful. Jade had placed plastic, but realistic looking butterflies in the flower arrangements. Several floating candles that were lit provided elegance on each table. There were three mocha colored board room like tables that were covered with off-white tablecloths. The first table contained fruit trays and trays with assorted cheese and crackers. Different flavours of beverages with plastic glasses could also be found on this table, as well as napkins. The last table contained all the sweets including peanut butter balls, date squares, almond biscotti, and amaretto cookies. Small little plates were provided for individuals to help themselves. There were also individual small clear bags filled with jellybeans in a large bowl. Kim had done a wonderful job with the finger food trays. The middle table had a beautiful 8 x 11inch picture of Skylar. Surrounding this picture were frames with multiple pictures of Skylar at different ages doing various activities. There were graduation photos, photos at the beach, and trips she had taken. The room looked beautiful. Both, Jade, and Kim were pleased.

"Now we just have to get through the next two hours, Jade said."

"We'll get through it together Jade." Kim reassured her.

Jade couldn't believe all the people that came to pay their respects. Skylar was well liked and loved. Besides her colleagues at the hospital, there were friends from outside the hospital, which must have found out about the celebration from people at the hospital.

Jade had seen Mark and his partner come in and just wander around. His partner approached her, "Ms. Rose, Detective Ross and I aren't here to cause any problems, we just want to observe the people that are coming and going."

"I have no problem with that Detective Shapiro. Please help yourself to the food. Oh, detective I would like to know when I can get back into my sister's apartment. I need to deal with her personal belongings before I go home."

"I understand. I believe we have taken all that we need into evidence from the apartment. CSI technicians have fingerprinted the apartment, as well as taken numerous photos. If I'm not mistaken, it has been cleaned up. However, I will make sure that you can re-enter."

"Thank you, detective."

Shapiro began walking back to where Ross was. Jade saw him noticing her, the same way she was noticing him.

"Her thoughts were interrupted when she heard a voice calling her name. "Ms. Rose how are you this evening? Lovely celebration for your sister."

"Thank you, Dr. Martins and thank you for coming. I'm fine. Feeling much better thank you."

"So glad to hear it. Gave us quite a scare the other day. I wanted to call you to inquire as to how you were feeling but I didn't know how you would react to that. I didn't want to be unprofessional or intrusive."

"I don't have many friends here in Sudbury, and now with my sister gone, I have no family. I would have welcomed the inquiry Dr. Martins."

"How did you get here this evening. May I give you a ride back to your hotel?"

"I would appreciate that. I didn't want to drive because I didn't know what state of mind I would be in after the celebration. I'm heart broken of course, to have lost my sister, but so happy to see she was so loved by her colleagues and friends. She truly had a good life here."

"Unfortunately, I didn't know your sister well. I wish I did. We worked in different areas of the ER. Please take your time Ms. Rose, I will wait as long as needed."

"Dr. Martins, please call me Jade."

"Then please call me, Rodney."

Ross was close enough to hear the entire conversation between Jade and the good doctor. He was hitting on her. "I should be the one driving her back to the hotel, not Dr. Martins." Ross thought.

Before he did something stupid, Shapiro asked "you see anything out of sorts, anybody that looks out of place or lurking around?"

"No, I didn't see anything like that." Ross responded.

"Well, how would you? All you've been doing is staring at Jade."

"I'm sorry partner. I can't seem to get my shit together when I'm around her. Now, its starting to affect my work."

"You're fine. You need to talk to her and get everything out in the open. That will put everything into perspective. You know who I didn't see here tonight?"

"Who's that?"

"Mr. No strings attached. Morgan Sinclair. You would figure they enjoyed each other's company. Why not pay your respects?" Shapiro was curious.

"Didn't you say that he was a real piece of work when you interviewed him? Cold as ice." Ross reminded him.

"You're right, he was a real piece of work."

Ross couldn't take his eyes off Jade all evening. The celebration had ended at eight p.m. Jade enjoyed meeting many of Skylar's friends. They had kind words to say about her sister. There were few people that came in alone. It seemed like they all knew each other. There were no wanders. Jade and Kim, along with several of Kim's friends helped clean up and pack the photo frames in no time. Kim took two of the floral arrangements back to her place and Jade thought she would take one back to her hotel room, along with the photos. Ms. Lasalle took the last floral arrangement. Ross watched as the Doc helped Jade got into the passenger seat of his white Lexus. He was driving her back to the hotel and helping her bring the flowers and photos back to her hotel room. Ross just sighed. He could kick himself in the ass for being such a jerk.

"Thank you for the ride and for helping me bring all of this back to the hotel. I really appreciate it, Rodney."

"My pleasure Jade, its on my way. No worries. I was wondering if you would like to have dinner with me tomorrow night?"

"I would like that. Thank you, Rodney."

"I will pick you up at seven p.m. tomorrow evening."

"See you tomorrow evening Rodney. Goodnight."

"Goodnight Jade."

Jade shut the hotel room door as Dr. Martins turned to walk towards the elevator. She would rather be going out to dinner with Ross, but he's made it clear he doesn't want anything to do with her. So, she thought, I need to move on. He didn't even make any attempt to come and talk with me tonight.

"Jade's phone rang. "I know its late, but I had to call. Tonight, was beautiful," Kim said. "Thank you for asking me to be a part of it!"

"Thank you, Kim, for helping me put it together. I have your photos for you. I will bring them over soon, okay?"

"No problem. I'm working the next two nights, then off for two and back on days for two. Take care."

"Got it," Jade said. "Take care."

Jade was tired. She needed to go to bed. She needed to start putting her sister's affairs in order. She was going to start by speaking with Skylar's landlord.

Ross finally got home. He and Shapiro didn't leave the hospital until almost nine-thirty p.m. They wanted to make sure there were no stragglers lurking around after the celebration. He couldn't stop thinking about Jade. She looked beautiful in that wine-colored dress. The way it flowed when she moved, well every man in the room couldn't take their eyes off her. Those stilettoes made it look like her legs went on forever. Her hair looked messy, like she had just had sex. She was the most beautiful woman he had ever seen. God, he was getting a hard on just thinking about her. He needed to get some sleep, something that has eluded him since he slept with Jade. He thought, Jade isn't the type of woman you can sleep with and forget.

He said to himself, "she is unforgettable." He was going to talk to her. He just didn't know when or what exactly he was going to say.

CHAPTER 16

Ross and Shapiro were at the station going over what they had so far, which wasn't much.

Shapiro commented on Ryder Campbell's alibi. "His alibi is solid. I have photos of him at the wake and cemetery and about fifty invited guests that will swear under oath that he was at the funeral. We have statements from nurses and doctors that explained he was at the hospital at his father's bedside as he was dying. The Fairmont confirmed he was there and checked out on June 30th."

"The background check on Campbell yielded nothing. The guy is squeaky clean. He graduated with honors from Victoria High School in British Columbia. Was top of his class in Business at Western University in London, Ontario. He's a self-made millionaire. He's never been married and has no children. Has only one sister and a nephew. Campbell Enterprises does business all over the world and has homes and offices in Toronto, Montreal, and Rome. I'm going to continue to dig." Ross confirmed.

"With regards to Judge Hamilton, well we know he's married and has been for thirty-five years to Claire, (nee Lepage). They have three children, two daughters and one son. They are all married. The Judge and his wife have five grandchildren. He graduated from York University at the age of twenty-six and was called to the bar a year later. He was an attorney with his own practice in family law, a crown attorney and became a provincial Judge fifteen years ago. From what I can see, he is more of a family man. I want to find out what he was doing before he became an attorney. "Ross said.

"A family man that made time for an escort." Shapiro added. "I guess there could be worse things."

Ross asked, "Did anything more come out of the victim's financials?"

"Nothing else. She wasn't in debt; school loans were paid; her car was paid off and rent was paid on time. She had tens of thousands of dollars in a separate bank account, other than the one she used regularly. Now that money belongs to Jade. Besides the financials, the fingerprints the techs discovered yielded nothing. The prints belonged to people that frequented the victim's home such as Kim Marshall, Morgan Sinclair, and Jade."

"Jade's fingerprints are in the system?" Ross was surprised.

"They sure are. As a chef she had to have a fingerprint check done at one time or another.

"Ross what are your feelings about this case? Do you think it is someone she knew or worked with? Do you think her being an escort got her killed? Could it be someone she pissed off? Shapiro valued his opinion.

"It was someone she knew. Jade explained when we first met her, her sister was adamant about locking doors. She wouldn't have opened the door to a total stranger. No one knew she was an escort except for Kim, I think. I don't think it has to do with her being an escort. Maybe she pissed someone off. She was having occasional sex. Maybe, one of the men she was having occasional sex with, wanted more and she didn't and that may have pissed the person off."

Shapiro agreed with Ross.

"I wonder if Kim was the only one that knew she was an escort. Could there possibly have been someone else that may have known and didn't agree with what she was doing? How did the killer lure the victim out of her apartment? Did the Skylar go voluntarily? Dr. Lind found some kind of sedative in her system. How is it that her nosy neighbour didn't see any of this? There's still unanswered questions." Ross was going to find out.

"Shapiro do you mind continuing the background check on Judge Hamilton, while I pay Kim and the nosy neighbour another visit?"

"No, you go right on ahead. You know I like doing the checking part better than asking questions part."

"Great, Ross grabbed his jacket. He was going to speak with Ms. Lipton."

It was one p.m. when Ross arrived at the apartment complex and noticed the police caution tape was removed. "I guess the apartment was released and cleared and can be entered again, he said to himself. Shapiro said he would call Jade to let her know."

He knocked on Ms. Lipton's apartment door twice before she answered. "Hello Ms. Lipton. I'm Detective Ross. I questioned you about a week ago, regarding Ms. Rose."

"Yes, I remember. What can I do for you Detective Ross?"

"I need to ask you a few more questions if you have a minute."

"Of course, anything to assist. That poor girl. I still can't believe someone killed her. Pretty little thing."

"Did you see or hear anything out of the ordinary from Ms. Roses' apartment a couple of days prior to June 29th? Any yelling, talking, screaming, her leaving with someone against her will? Anything out of the ordinary?

"Detective Ross, I wasn't home from June 26 to June 29. I arrived home the afternoon of the 29th. My sister had a knee replacement a few days prior, and I was staying with her to help her out for a couple of days. You know like picking up her prescriptions, laundry, cleaning the house, and making meals. If you need to call her now. She will tell you."

"No, Ms. Lipton that won't be necessary. Thank you for your time."

Ross was hoping he would have better luck with Kim Marshall. He was heading there next.

Jade had spoken with a rental manager at TBS Property Management. They owned the apartment complex her sister lived in. Just before she had spoken to the rental manager, she received a call from Detective Shapiro informing her, her sister's apartment had been released and can now be entered.

Ms. Carriere expressed her condolences on behalf of the management team. "Please take the rest of the month to pack your sister's belongings. Will you need a key?"

"Thank you for your kindness. No, I have a spare key which I will return to you when I have finished packing and moving my sister's belongings."

Ross was about to leave the apartment complex when he saw Jade walking up the walkway to her sister's apartment. She must have been informed; the apartment had been released. They had to cross each other, along the walkway.

"Hello Jade." Ross looked directly at her. As usual, she looked great.

Jade refused to look at him and only said, "detective."

"Someone informed you the apartment had been released."

She had her back to him, putting the key into the door lock. "Detective Shapiro was kind enough to call me." She walked in and shut the door without say anything else or looking back at him.

Ross was left there standing alone on the walkway just staring at the closed door. Now he was mad. This is going to stop, and it stops tonight. He was going over to the hotel this evening. They needed to talk. He couldn't do this anymore. Ross left to speak with Kim.

Jade closed the door on him and leaned her back against the closed door. She closed the door quickly because she didn't want him to see her crying. Coming back to her sister's apartment and having to go through all her belongings was hard enough, but to see him. Her heart was truly broken now. She couldn't do this now. She sat and wept for the loss of her sister and the man she had fallen in love with.

Ross had questioned Kim about whether anyone else was privy to the fact that the victim was an escort.

"I was the only one she told. No one else knew. You had to know Skylar. I was the only one that knew, and I never told anyone, except for you and just recently, Jade. If anyone else knew, then they must have recognized her some how, at some point. Why do you ask?

"Thanks for your time, Kim."

"Detective Ross, can I tell you something that's not related to the case?"

Ross gave her a curious look. "Sure, what is it"

"This is none of my business, but her goes. Jade has it bad for you! That's why she won't talk to you. I don't' know what happened but whatever it was, you hurt her. She didn't confide in me or anything, but I could tell something happened between you two, the last time you came to my house. Just thought you should know. If you need to ask me anything else, I'm working night shift tonight and tomorrow night."

"Thanks for your help, Kim."

Ross left and walked to his car. He knew he had hurt her. He needed to fix things. Tonight, he thought. Tonight.

CHAPTER 17

JADE DIDN'T WANT TO BE here tonight. The restaurant was beautiful with Its Italian décor, Italian music playing quietly in the back ground and the smell of home-made bread. Dr. Martins was a gentleman; however, the conversation was less than interesting. Her heart just wasn't in it.

"Jade are you alright? You seem a million miles away."

"My sister's apartment was released today. I went over to gauge what needed to be done and I was overcome with emotion. I am having such a tough time; I can't seem to think straight, my thoughts are off in every direction. I'm so sorry Rodney but I'm afraid I won't be much good company this evening. Would you mind driving me back to the hotel?"

"Of course not, I can stay with you, if you would like."

"No, that won't be necessary, but thank you."

Dr. Martins drove her back and there was little conversation between the two. "I'm worried about you Jade. Are you sure you don't need me to stay, even for a little while? Is there someone I can call for you?"

"Thank you, Rodney, I'll be fine. I just need time to rest is all, Goodnight."

"Goodnight Jade. Hope you feel better. I'll call you soon."

Jade walked back to her hotel room. She was so relieved. She just didn't want to be with Rodney. Part of it was being at Skylar's apartment, but it was mostly seeing Mark today. She hadn't even taken off her stilettos when there was a knock on the door. She assumed it was Rodney, so she opened it without looking through the peephole. Mark walked right in.

"We need to talk." He wasn't leaving.

Her defenses went up. "Get out. I don't want to talk to you. I have nothing to say to you."

"Well, I have lots to say to you Jade. So shut the door. I'm not leaving until I've said what I came here to say."

"I don't care about what you have to say. I don't want to do this." She let go of the door, turned to pick up her purse and went for the door again, to leave. He grabbed her and shut the door.

He pinned her against the closed door. She was trying to get out of his hold, but she was no match for his strength. He pinned her arms above her head as she was pushing at him with her hands, in the hopes that he would release her. "Stop this and listen to me." He demanded.

They were a couple of inches apart, facing each other. There was fire in her blue eyes, and he knew he was in for a fight, but she was worth fighting for. She was breathing heavy, her chest rising high to touch his. She smelled wonderful. He couldn't believe he was getting hard.

"Let me go Mark and get the hell out of my room. I have nothing to say to you and I don't care what you have to say. There's nothing you can say. You hurt me. You got what you wanted, and then I didn't hear from you. There was no phone call from you. You couldn't even talk to me at my sister's Celebration of Life. Nothing. Now let me go dammit! Let me go!"

He looked directly at her. "Jade, I'm crazy about you! I've been crazy about you since the first time we had dinner together. After we spent the night together, I was lost. I was afraid of getting close to you. I can't watch you walk away and go home. I thought it would be best if I just ignored you, forgot about you but I couldn't do it anymore. Every time I saw you, I just wanted to wrap my arms around you and kiss you. I can't sleep. I don't eat. I'm irritable. You're all I think about."

Jade had stopped fighting and trying to free herself. She had tears in her eyes. She wanted to hear him say it over and over. He was crazy about her. She just looked at him.

He looked at her and let her arms go but continued to have her lightly pinned against the door. "I'm so sorry baby. So sorry. I wish I can take the pain I've caused you, all back, but I can't."

Mark continued to look at her. He took the back of his thumb and wiped away a tear from her eye. "Please say something Jade. I've said everything I came here to say. Even if you still don't want to talk to me, at least I got to say what I came here to say."

Jade continued to look at him and still wasn't talking. She had composed herself. Mark was starting to move away. He didn't want to stay, if she didn't want him here after he told her what he came here to say. As he began moving away, she cupped his face with both hands and kissed him. He responded by deepening the kiss.

"Say it again Mark."

"I'm crazy, crazy about you. I want you and only you Jade."

"Mark are you okay." Jade noticed he was just staring at her.

"I'm fine, really good right now. I just want to look at you. I need to look at you. You're beautiful, absolutely beautiful."

He moved closer to her. She was wearing a black body-hugging dress with those black stilettos, which drove him crazy the night before. She was trying to take her shoes off, and he stopped her.

"Leave those sexy shoes on, I'll take them off for you, later."

He began kissing her lightly and caressing her back. He knew her body by memory, every curve. He moved his hands to the curves of her ass, and he deepened the kiss. He brought her closer to him, grinding his hard on into her and kissed her hard. He began undressing her. She was wearing matching bra and panties in black lace and with those black stilettoes on, she was the sexiest woman he had ever seen. She saw the want in his eyes. He completely undressed her and touched her sex. She was wet and ready.

"Mark that feels wonderful." She touched his erection through his pants. He groaned. She looked at him and slowly positioned herself to take in the length of his erection. She undid his belt and lowered the zipper to his pants. She slowly reached in and wrapped his shaft with one hand and took in his full length. Mark groaned with pleasure. He loved her mouth.

A few minutes later she stopped, looking up at him with want. He guided her back to the bed and for a while just wanted to kiss her. He devoured her mouth. He caressed her face and began kissing her neck, moving down to her breasts, further down to her abdomen and then he kissed her moist area. Jade cried out. Mark touched her with his tongue and didn't stop. Jade had her hands in his hair, squirming and moaning. He loved making her squirm. It drove him nuts. He kept this up until she orgasmed. Jade came unraveled, crying out his name. Her skin glowing with moisture.

She was breathing heavy when she said, "I want you, Mark."

That's all he needed to hear. He covered his erection with a condom and mounted her. Mark penetrated her, moving slowly at first then faster. Jade was in heaven, feeling him move in and out, while he was fondling and suckling her breasts. She loved his touch on her body and him being inside her. They enjoyed each other completely. Then he touched her moist area while moving in and out, causing Jade to completely come apart. He felt her pelvic muscles contracting causing him to find his release. His whole body shook. He just fell beside her in bed. Both were very satisfied.

He was just staring at her, while she was lying on her stomach with her eyes closed, with her stilettoes still on. "You are unbelievable Jade. I can't get enough of you. You rest. I'm not done with you yet baby. Afterall, you still have your stilettoes on."

"She started laughing. You're not so bad yourself. I was hoping we weren't done just yet."

"Stop talking that way or you won't be able to rest." He warned.

She stuck out the tip of her tongue and began moving it along her upper lip and then lower lip. "Anytime you're ready, so am I."

He wanted her to lie on him. "Come over to me. Lie on me." She moved closer, putting her head and arm on his chest. He could hear her breathing evenly. Her gorgeous hair was everywhere. He wrapped his arm around her. "Why were you all dressed up tonight? You looked nice."

She looked up at him, "Dr. Martins asked me out to dinner last night."

"And you said you would go?"

"I did. Afterall, its not like you were showing any interest in me." Just before we were going to order, I wanted to come home. After going to Skylar's apartment and going through some of her things and seeing you there, I just didn't feel like being with him. I wanted to be with you."

"Jade, I wanted to be with you too, but I knew you were too upset with me. I didn't want to cause you any more pain. I don't blame you for being angry at me. I was angry at myself for being a jerk."

She continued to look at him, while moving her fingers through his chest hairs, "you were definitely being a jerk. What were you so afraid of?"

"I've never felt the way I feel about you, about any woman. I was and still am afraid of you leaving. At some point you are going home. Aren't you? Then what?"

"Remember when I told you that I was going to talk to Skylar about moving to Sudbury?"

"Sure, I remember."

"Well, I'm still thinking about it. I need a change. I feel closer to my sister here. I know that she's gone but I feel her near me, here. I don't have anyone in the Sault. I have my job. A job I can do anywhere. I'm not sure yet, but perhaps you can persuade me to stay."

He looked down at her pretty face and kissed her. "Oh, I'm going to enjoy persuading you. I want you to stay with me, while you're here. My place isn't big but its clean and comfortable."

"Thank you but no Mark. Believe me I want to, but you need to concentrate on finding my sister's killer. I will never be whole until her killer is found. I think I will just be a distraction. Something, you don't need. I hope you understand."

"Oh, I understand that you will be a distraction, but you're right. I promise you; we will find your sister's killer. We are still following up on leads."

"I know you can't talk to me about the leads because the investigation is ongoing. I hope the killer is found soon."

It was almost nine-thirty p.m. "Let's order room service. You're going to need your strength, Jade." The look of desire was clearly in his eyes.

CHAPTER 18

S͟HAPIRO WAS ALREADY IN THE office when Ross arrived. Shapiro could tell from Ross' face that he was in a particularly good mood. "Wonderful, you finally talked to her."

"Holy shit, do you know everything, Shapiro?"

"I know that look. I've had it on my face after…. well, you know."

"We had a nice long talk after she nearly smacked the crap out of me, which I deserved."

Ross thought, we did way more than just talk. He didn't want to leave her this morning. He was going to see her later this evening. She was going to meet him at his place. He left his keys with her. She had a couple of things to do today.

"Any new developments on the case?"

"I'm still looking into Judge Hamilton's background. Its difficult trying to get information about a Judge. They are very well protected and rightfully so. There are crazy people every where."

"So, we still got nothing on this case?

Ross' cell phone started ringing. From the caller ID, it was Dr. Lind at the morgue. "Hey Doc."

"Detective Ross, a pubic hair was found on our victim, which didn't belong to her. The Forensic Lab in Toronto got a profile from it, however there was no match in the Canadian National DNA database or CODIS (Combined DNA Index System)."

"Well, that's good news, now we just have to find the person that matches the profile. Thanks Doc."

Ross told his partner about the pubic hair found. "We don't have probable cause to obtain a warrant for DNA swabs from Judge Hamilton and Ryder Campbell." Shapiro said.

Ross thought about it. "You're right but we can ask for them to provide us with one voluntarily and see what happens."

Shapiro was already on the phone with Ryder Campbell. "Mr. Campbell, this is Detective Shapiro. I am calling in hopes that you would voluntarily give us a DNA sample. The reason I am asking for it, is to exclude you as a suspect. Your alibi did checkout, but this would positively exclude you. Great then, give me a call when you get back to town."

Shapiro explained that Mr. Campbell is out of the country and won't be back to Sudbury for another two weeks. He will call when he is back and doesn't have a problem giving us a DNA sample.

"Wonderful, then that means Judge Hamilton is the only one that needs to be called." Ross said.

Shapiro was looking at Ross with that "you better get on it look."

"Fine, I'll call him. I owe you anyway."

"Yes, you do Ross and don't think that I'll ever forget it. This is just the tip of the iceberg." Shapiro was laughing.

"Judge Hamilton, this is Detective Ross. I was hoping that you would voluntarily to give us a sample of your DNA. Your alibi checked out, but a sample would positively rule you out as a suspect." Shapiro could hear a very upset Judge on the phone." I understand sir. Thank you for your time."

"No way is he volunteering a DNA sample. He said if we want it, then get a warrant. He said, he was being very cooperative up until now and this was the last straw. Any further questions, can go through his lawyer."

Macy was working the streets tonight. It was a warm July evening. She was under the Bridge of Nations with Jaz, her best friend. Business was slow, despite the decent weather. A john approached her in a black sedan and tinted windows.

"You up for some fun?" He offered her a lot of money for two hours of her time.

"You bet sweetheart." She took him back to the hotel she frequents with johns. He gave her money to pay for he hotel. He didn't want to be seen.

The room looked more like an old shack. It had a bed that had more lumps than a boxer after a fight, the comforter was stained with God knows what, and a table with a couple of lawn chairs and a lamp were in the corner. It smelled like dirty socks, and it was hot. There was no air conditioning. The bath tub had mold and the toilet was dirty. Once in the room, Macy quickly got undressed, which took no time at all cause all she was wearing was a tight dress and stilettoes. She went to him and started touching him.

"Ready to have fun? He asked her.

"Sure thing."

While having sex with Macy, he thought, there's nothing lady like about her. There's no softness to her. She was a hard ass all the way around.

"You having fun baby, cause I am," Macy said.

This isn't about you bitch. Its about me. I don't care if you're having fun, he thought.

He just laughed. "Well, that's good because you're not going anywhere for a while. I'm not done with you just yet."

"Sure baby, anything you want."

He stopped abruptly. *"I want to watch you please yourself on the table. Can you do that?"*

"Oh yeah, baby I can do that. No problem."

He left the bed to sit in a chair by the table. Macy got off the bed and laid down on the table. She began masturbating while he watched. *She's enjoying herself; I don't like it. This isn't about her. It's about me, he thought.*

"She continued to masturbate. This is just for you baby." Macy said while looking at him in a sultry way.

He found her sultry look disgusting. "Stop and get off the table. Get back on the bed and spread them wide, he ordered."

He covered his shaft with a new condom and penetrated her, moving with fast even rhythm.

He knew she was on the verge of orgasm. *"I can feel you coming apart slut."*

He kept moving without stopping. Macy found her release and his orgasm soon followed causing his entire body to shake.

Macy had had enough of this guy's crap. "Don't call me a slut. My release had nothing to do with you, asshole."

"Thanks for this, slut. That's all your good for, you know that, right."

"Don't talk to me that way. What's your problem? Did your girlfriend leave you for another guy with a bigger dick?"

From where he was standing, he came over and slapped her across the face. *"You don't know anything about me. You're a stupid slut."*

"Screw you asshole, I'm out of here. I've had better than you. You'll never have me again for all the money in the world." She knew she shouldn't care about what a john says, but after the way she'd been treated by guys like him her whole life, no way was she going to kiss his ass. She got dressed and walked out. She was heading home.

Macy was just trying to focus when she came to. Her eyes wouldn't say open. She felt like an elastic band. She was thirsty, had a dry mouth and was nauseated. She didn't know where she was or how she got here. Her ankles and wrists were tied with rope and the bindings were starting to bruise her skin. Her skin was on fire. The place smelled of urine and so did this mattress she was sitting on. It was a dungeon. Nothing here but this mattress, a small table with nothing on it and a garbage can. There was little light. "How the hell did I get here? Why am I here? Answer me, whoever you are." she said out loud.

She needed to get the hell out of here. She was starting to remember bits and pieces. She remembered telling off some john last night for calling her a slut. Was it him? The door rattled, and then opened. A bright light came on that blinded her and someone was coming down the stairs. She recognized him. It was the asshole from last night, she thought.

"Why are you doing this because I told you off last night? You weren't exactly being a nice guy yourself. You kept calling me a slut. Where am I anyway? This place is like a dungeon."

"Why am I doing this because you're a slut who has a big mouth and doesn't know when to shut up, that's why. You told me you would never screw me again for all the money in the world. Someone like you is going to turn down a shit load of money, because she was called a slut. You screw men for money and you're rejecting me because I called you a slut. You will screw me."

Even if he was going to kill her, she was going out her way, not crying or begging this guy. "You're an asshole. Let's get this over with."

After he was done having sex with her, he threw the used condom in the garbage can near by. She just closed her eyes and looked away. He went up the stairs, shut the lights off and locked the door. Macy knew she was going to die. She knew what she had to do.

Officer Tilley walked over to Ross' desk, "Jaz is here, and she wants to speak with you."

Ross thought, what is Jaz doing here? I don't work sex crimes anymore. He looked at her and she looked scared. "Ross, Macy is missing. She didn't come home this morning. She always comes home."

Macy and Jaz weren't even twenty years old and had been prostitutes since they were sixteen. At least that's when Ross met them. Jaz was blond and blue eyed. She was petite but could hold her own. She wore a lot of makeup and had a nose ring and tattoos above her right and left breast. Macy had dark hair and dark eyes. He remembers, her hair was wavy and mid back in length. Macy was full figured. She had tattoos but he couldn't remember where. She had a foul mouth and didn't take any crap from anybody. Both girls had a terrible home life and had fallen through the cracks. Jaz started doing drugs with her mother at an early age and mommy dearest got her into prostitution. Her mother die from an overdose. Macy was sexually abused by her stepfather and his brother. They thought it was fun to take turns. The girls looked out for each other. Ross really felt for Jaz right now.

"Jaz calm down. Maybe she's still working." Ross thought."

"No fucking way, Ross. She told me, one more trick and she was walking home. I left before her. I wasn't feeling good. Last time I saw her was one this morning. She wouldn't be with a john this whole time. Something has happened."

"When you saw her last, what was she doing?"

"She was talking to this john in a black sedan. I saw her get into his car."

"A black sedan." Ross repeated and looked at his partner. "Did you get a licence plate maybe?

"Really, Ross. I don't look at licence plates"

Shapiro introduced himself to Jaz. "What was she wearing last night."

Jaz had to think about it. "She had on a body-hugging dress with stilettos. I think the dress was a navy blue and the shoes were black. She wasn't wearing a bra or underwear. What's the point?"

"Jaz I'm going to take all your information and pass this on to sex crimes division. They will investigate it. That's the best I can do. I am working on a murder case right now.

"Fine as long as someone starts looking for her. I'll tell you what you want to know."

Ross took all of the information Jaz had given him and transferred it to sex crimes division. Detectives Kevin Moore and Bill Gladstone were going to look into it. Ross had worked with both gentlemen. They were good guys and good cops.

Ross and Shapiro explained to both Moore and Gladstone that the case they are working on may be connected. Their murder victim was a high-priced escort and was being possibly stalked by someone in a black sedan. Macy was a street walker who was telling someone in a black sedan to get lost. The cases are different but have similarities, Ross thought.

"We find out anything, we'll let you know." Moore said.

Ross and Shapiro sat down at their desks and were thinking the same thing. Shapiro voiced it out loud, "is this guy after sex workers, be it high-priced or street walkers?"

"I don't know, but if the cases are connected, our job just got harder.

Ross was sitting at his desk having lunch and going through his notes on the case. His thoughts went to Jade. She was incredible. He more than liked her. He knew he was falling in love with her, but he just couldn't say it to her. He felt it was too soon. They had only known each other for a couple weeks. She was thinking of moving here and Ross was going to persuade her to stay. He smiled and thought about the multiple ways he could persuade her.

Jade had woken up with a smile on her face. He may be crazy about me, but she was in love with him. She was planning to find a job here. She wanted to move here regardless of her relationship with Mark. She felt closer to her sister here. There were two Italian restaurants she wanted to apply to as a chef and a teaching position in Culinary Arts at the community college. She didn't tell Mark about the positions because she didn't want him to get his hopes up. Jade didn't' want to get her hopes up. She was going to do what she needed to do and hope for the best. She was excited about going to Mark's place. He didn't know it, but she was going to cook for him tonight. She had packed an overnight bag with sexy lingerie. She had her resumes prepared and her bag in hand when her cell phone rang.

"Hello"

"Jade, it's Rodney. How are you feeling this morning?"

"Rodney, hello. I'm much better, thank you. I am sorry for last night."

"Would you like to continue this evening, where we left off last evening?"

"I'm afraid I can't Rodney. Honestly, I shouldn't have accepted your offer for dinner. I guess when I accepted, I was vulnerable and lonely. There is still so much I have to do regarding my sister's affairs. A friend is helping me get through things. I am sorry Rodney."

"Well, I hope it all works out with your sister's affairs. You take care of yourself.

"You as well, Rodney."

Jade needed to drop off the resumes before the three-p.m. deadline. She was hoping to be considered for the teaching position. Afterwards she had to go grocery shopping for dinner this evening.

Detectives Moore and Gladstone canvased the area under the bridge of nations and found nothing. No one even knew Macy was missing. They did see her last evening but that was it. Jaz had explained which way Macy usually walked home. In a back alley, near the apartment she and Jaz shared, the detectives found a black sweater and purse. Jaz confirmed both belonged to Macy.

"If you look in the inside zippered pocket, you will find a picture of her and I. I have the same picture in my purse. You'll also find mace." Jaz said.

It was Macy's purse. Jaz broke down. "Where is she? She wouldn't just leave her purse. I know she's in trouble. Please find her, please."

Jade had arrived at Mark's place. She had groceries that needed to be put away. She put her night bag in the bedroom. She was going to spend the night. She had no intention of leaving. Looking around, it was a decent size, clean but plain. It could use a woman's touch and some color, otherwise it was pleasant. The living room had a large brown sectional which surrounded a square coffee table. The one bedroom had a black king size bed covered with a white comforter. The kitchen had a dark colored pub set with matching stools. Jade opened the fridge and just stared. The man had nothing in his fridge. That told her, he was never at home. She decided she was going to be nosey and look in the cupboards for salt and pepper she needed for the meal. There was absolutely nothing here. She needed to go back out to the grocery store. She needed a bottle of wine, so she was also going to the wine store. She didn't have much time.

Ross was heading home to Jade. He couldn't wait to see her. He couldn't wait to kiss her. As he was leaving, he stopped to talk to Moore and Gladstone. "Any more news on Macy?"

Gladstone just nodded. "We got nothing besides finding her sweater and purse. We're thinking this was a surprise abduction. If she had gone willingly, she would have taken her purse and sweater. We got no witnesses, no nothing. It doesn't look good. The only good thing is that she hasn't been found dead."

"No news is good news. Gentlemen have a good evening."

CHAPTER 19

At her sister's Celebration of Life, she was beautiful and elegant. I knew where she was staying while in town. I thought she was different, but she was like her sister, a slut. Last night, she was brought back to the hotel by one man and then he saw another man going to her room. It was that detective. It obviously, wasn't business because he stayed all night. I spent the night in my car. He was sleeping with her, no doubt. I wonder who else she's sleeping with. Let's see who's joining her tonight. He checked the hotel parking lot and didn't notice her car. She should be back soon. I've got no where to go so I'll wait for the slut.

Jade had time to take a shower. She was dressed casually with a tee shirt and denim mini skirt on. Dinner was almost ready, and the table was set. No candles. Ross didn't strike her as a candles kind of guy. Ross just needed to get home. She heard the door unlock and then open.

"Those legs go on, forever, don't they? Hi baby."

"Hi yourself."

Ross looked at the table and something smelled wonderful. "What did you do?"

"I wanted to cook you dinner. Afterall, that's what I do."

"Really, that's great. I can't remember the last time I had a home cooked meal."

He went over to her and wrapped his arms around her waist and kissed her like he hadn't seen her in years. She responded by wrapping her arms around his neck and kissed him back.

"Can we go right to dessert?" he said.

"No, now let's sit down and have dinner. We can talk a little."

"What are we going to talk about?"

"Whatever. A little of this. A little of that."

Jade had prepared spinach and ricotta cannelloni with garlic, rosemary, and herb focaccia for supper and a beautiful chocolate, hazelnut torte with amaretto coffee for dessert. She had chosen a crisp Pinot Grigio white wine to go with supper.

"That was great Jade. You can cook babe!"

"Thank you. Would you like more wine, Mark?"

"Sure. I would like to wait a while for dessert. Its early."

"That sounds fine. We can save it for tomorrow if you want. The cannelloni fills me up anyway.

"Tomorrow? Are you going to be here tomorrow Jade?"

"I guess that would depend on you Mark."

"I would like to take you out for a nice dinner and then go back to the hotel. Is that okay with you, Jade?"

Jade wondered why he didn't want to come back to his apartment. "Sounds like a plan. What will we do with the torte?"

"Don't worry about the torte Jade. We'll eat it. No worries."

Jade gave him a curious look but didn't ask.

"So, what did you do today?

"Not very much. Grocery shopping and errands. I'm looking into something, but I don't want to jinx it, so I don't want to talk about it right now. If it works out, I'll be more than happy to share the news, of course. Dr. Martins called today. He was wondering how I was doing after cutting our date short last evening."

"Is that all he asked?"

"No, he wondered if we could pick up where we left off last evening."

"He did, did he. He's persistent."

"Mark, he was just being considerate. I told him I have too much on my plate right now and it would be best for me to concentrate on dealing with my sister's affairs and clearing out her apartment. He understood."

"Is that what you plan on doing tomorrow, going to your sister's place?"

"I can't keep avoiding the inevitable. It has to be done. I need closure. Taking care of her affairs will be part of it, finding her killer will be the other part.

"Jade I can't talk about an open investigation."

"Mark, I didn't ask for any information about my sister's case. I'm just telling you what I need."

"I know honey. I just hope you get the closure you need."

It was eight p.m. by the time they had finished drinking their glasses of wine. Mark needed to take a shower. He asked Jade to join him, but she had just had one before he got home. Jade cleaned up the kitchen, meanwhile. When he came out of the shower, he had a towel wrapped around his hips. His hair and skin were still damp. The hairs on his chest appeared to be glistening. He didn't shave. He liked the 5 o'clock shadow and Jade thought, it was sexy as all hell. He walked towards her and wrapped his arms around her. She could feel he was hard underneath that towel.

"Jade come with me." He escorted her to the bedroom.

She wanted a minute to wash up and slip into something more comfortable. "I'll be there in a minute, and she picked up her night bag and went to the bathroom."

"Take your time he told her. I have to go get something."

Jade came back to the room in a red lace bra and panty lingerie set. Mark was lying on the bed and when he saw her, he froze. He couldn't take his eyes off of her.

"I'll say it again, you're beautiful, Jade. Sexy, sexy, sexy. Come to me."

She went to him. She asked him, "what did you have to go and get?"

Then he showed her the torte. "I thought we could have fun with dessert."

They both laughed. Then he showed her how much he wanted her.

Ross and Jade had fun with the torte till midnight then they both fell asleep. It was eight a.m. and Ross had to get ready for work. He looked at Jade once he was up. She was nude under the sheet. He saw her red lace bra and panty on the floor and remembered what she looked like in it last night. Ross couldn't believe it, but he was getting hard just looking at her and the red lace lingerie. He couldn't get enough of this woman. He wanted more. She stirred for a bit.

"You going to work babe?"

"Yeah. I'll call you about dinner. I'm leaving my keys with you so you can lock up. I'll grab them from you when I see you later."

"Sounds good."

He kissed her and kissed her. He really wished he didn't have to go to work or could call in sick today but there was too much going on.

"I've got to go now, or I'll never leave."

"I'm going back to bed, "Jade said.

Ross got to work at nine a.m. Shapiro was staring at nothing. He had a blank stair, drinking a cup of coffee.

"You alright Shapiro?"

"No, I'm pissed because we have hit rock bottom with the Skylar Rose case. We're out of leads and we got nothing."

"Shapiro what does your gut tell you."

"My gut tells me that Judge Hamilton has something to do with this and he is untouchable at this point. Somehow, we need a sample of his DNA."

"Good luck with that," Ross said.

"Any news about Macy?"

"Nothing there either. She's been missing for approximately thirty hours. Jaz has already called this morning."

"Moore and Gladstone will turn up something. When street walkers disappear, it seems nobody sees anything.

Its unfortunate. I'm going to ask Jaz for a photo of Macy. Maybe the local media can help us."

"Sounds good. At least we're doing something productive," Shapiro said. "Right now, I feel useless."

You and me both, Ross thought.

CHAPTER 20

SHAPIRO AND ROSS WERE GOING over their notes again and working on angles when Ross' cell phone rang. It was Moore.

"Ross, we found Macy. Unfortunately, she's dead."

"Where?"

"Gladstone and I decided to go back out to the area where she was last seen. We found her halfway under the Bridge of Nations, near the tracks. We're waiting for the coroner."

"Thanks Gladstone. Are you going to inform Jaz afterwards?"

"Moore is on his way there now. She seems to like him more."

Ross informed Shapiro of Macy's death.

Dr. Lind arrived at the area under the Bridge of Nations. He noticed the area had been secured with police caution tape and the victim had been covered with a police standard drape. CSI investigators were collecting evidence and taking pictures. Macy was on her left side, with her hands bound in front her. Her wrists were bruised. Her dress was the only thing she had on. There were no shoes or jewelry. She appeared to be dishevelled and dehydrated. She had bruising on both sides of her face.

Dr. Lind completed a preliminary examination and tentatively concluded the victim had died from stab wounds. "I see two stab wounds to the abdomen. I will know more once I complete the autopsy. Liver temperature is 90.2 degrees Fahrenheit so I would say she has been dead approximately six hours. Her bindings and dress will have to be processed. She has some sticky residue all over her hands. We need to determine what that is. It looks like I have a busy day ahead of me." A CSI investigator placed a paper bag over the victims hands and bindings to protect the possible evidence on them. Paper didn't create moisture like plastic did.

"It looks like this is a secondary crime scene. There's no blood around except on the victim. She wasn't killed here." Gladstone said.

"It looks that way." Dr. Lind agreed.

Jade had gone back to her sister's apartment. She needed to get her affairs in order. There was no will. Jade was her next of kin. There was no one else. According to her lawyer she had to apply for a Certificate of Appointment of Estate Trustee without a Will, in order to be the representative for her sisters property and finances.

Jade was going to donate the furniture from the apartment to the Gemma House, an emergency shelter for abused women. When Skylar spoke about the abused women that came through the emergency department, her heart went out to them. This way even after her death, she is still doing something to help them. Jade was going to keep the pictures of her and Skylar. Perhaps, Kim would like the pictures of her and Skylar. Jade needed to call Kim and ask her if there was anything in the apartment that she wanted. Jade spent the next few hours boxing up books and nursing texts which she as going to donate to the city library. She decided to call Kim. There was no answer, so she left a message.

"Hey Kim, its Jade. I'm at Skylar's apartment. I was just wondering if you wanted to come over. I didn't know if there was something here that you'd want. Call me back when you have a minute."

Jade packed all of Skylar's clothes, except for the pieces that she wanted. She was going to donate the clothes to the Women's Centre. She threw out things like makeup, pillows, shower curtain, bathroom rugs, items in the medicine cabinet and food that by now was rotten. Jade went through all of the mail she found and threw out junk and kept the rest. There were a few bills that needed to be paid such as the cable and hydro. Jade had called and disconnected these already. She thought, a lot was accomplished today. Its almost two-thirty p.m. She looked around at the packed-up boxes and started to cry. Is this all our lives amount to is packed boxes? She said out loud "I miss you Skylar, I miss you little sister." She composed herself, took a few items with her, locked up and left. She would be back.

Moore and Gladstone were both walking into the station at about three p.m. They had come from the morgue. Dr. Lind still had a couple of hours with the body.

"How's Jaz," Ross asked.

Moore was shaking his head from side to side, "she's hysterical. That's the only way I can explain it. She would compose herself, then start talking about Macy, and become hysterical again. She called a friend to come over. When she got there, I left. Jaz told me; Macy's last name was Collins. She has no family or next of kin except for herself."

"Its going to be hard for Jaz for a long time. Those girls did everything together. Really, they only had each other." Ross said.

Moore and Gladstone started making their way to their desks, when Gladstone turned around to say, "Dr. Lind wanted us to give you a message. He wants to speak to both of you in the morgue."

Shapiro and Ross just looked at each other. "Thanks for letting us know." Ross said.

Shapiro and Ross made their way down to the morgue. Shapiro hated this place. It was cold and sterile. Here the conversation was one sided and the first person to tell their story was the victim, themselves.

Shapiro greeted Dr. Lind, "you wanted to speak to Ross and myself. Is that correct?" Ross was just looking at Macy on the cold, steel table. He thought, what a life this girl had. Its just not fair.

"Yes. I wanted to let you know that this murder victim has similarities to Skylar Rose."

"Macy Collin's death is most definitely a homicide?"

"She was killed by two fatal stab wounds to the abdomen puncturing her spleen and several blood vessels. She bled out. The stab wounds were caused by an eight-inch carving knife. The same as in the Skylar Rose case. This victim was sexually assaulted; however, I found no semen in the vaginal, oral, or anal cavity. Unlike Skylar Rose, this victim had semen all over her hands. The sticky substance on her hands was semen. It has been sent to the lab for processing. She had bruising to her face suggesting physical assault and just like Skylar Rose, the body had a faint smell of urine"

"If her hands were bound, how did she get semen on her hands? Its not like the killer would just hand it over to her, so he could be implicated or caught." Shapiro said.

"No, he wouldn't. But I knew Macy. She was tough as nails. She knew he was going to kill her, so she was going to make sure we would find out who he was. Her way of screwing him over. She probably got a hold of the used condom after he sexually assaulted her and somehow emptied the contents all over her hands. Macy was smarter than most people gave her credit for. She knew her hands would be looked at by the authorities. There was no way she was going to let him get away with what he did. She was going to make sure of that." Ross added.

Shapiro said out loud, "I looks like we possibly have two murders committed by the same person. We'll know as soon as the DNA comes back on the semen found on Macy's hands."

Both Ross and Dr. Lind agreed. "As soon as toxicology and DNA results come back, I'll call you," Dr. Lind advised.

He went back to the room," the dungeon" as that bitch, Macy called it. Well, she won't be saying anything to anyone from now on. What a mouth on her. She was a ball of fire. He hadn't noticed the garbage can was tipped over when he took Macy out of the room. He went over to it and saw the used condom on the floor with semen at the opening. He was immediately consumed with anger. He was so mad, his hands curled into fists, and he kicked the small table, sending it flying into the wall, breaking in half. He said out loud "that little bitch."

Ross had called Jade two hours earlier. He explained, "I'm picking you up at six p.m. and we are going to the Hour Glass Restaurant and Lounge for supper."

That was an hour and a half ago, she thought. Ross will be here in half hour. She just needed to get dressed. She was going to wear a black and grey lace top, off the shoulder with flared sleeves and a black split thigh pencil skirt with her famous black stilettos. Jade was going to talk to Mark about why he wanted to come back to the hotel and not go back to his place. The comment he made last night at his place, didn't sit well with her. After all he's the one that wanted her to stay at his place while she was in town. It didn't make any sense. She got dressed and just in time, as there was a knock on the door. She checked the peephole, it was Mark.

"Hi there. Come on in" she said.

"Hi honey. You look great."

She did. She was absolutely a vision. Skin that glowed, eyes that sparkled and hair, so shiny and wavy. In one word, "sexy."

"Thank you, Mark."

He moved closer to kiss and hug her. She was as soft as a gentle rain and smelled like a day at the beach. He wanted this everyday. "Ready to go?"

Well look at her. She's with the detective again. That's probably who she was with last night. No doubt at his place. They were probably enjoying each other in every which way possible. She didn't come back to the hotel. What about the doctor? How many men does she need?

Another slut just like her sister. She's like the others. She'll die like the others, soon. I hate him, but I hate her more.

The Hour Glass restaurant and lounge was a romantic place to dine. It was located in a beautifully renovated Victorian building in downtown Sudbury. Jade and Mark had enjoyed a delicious supper. She ordered the goat cheese stuffed chicken and he, the New York strip. A glass of red Cabernet Sauvignon accompanied dinner. Both had declined dessert and were enjoying the ambiance and beauty of the restaurant.

"Mark why aren't we going back to your place? Why did you want to go back to the hotel? A couple of days ago you wanted me to stay with you until I needed to go home and last night you wanted to come back to the hotel. I don't understand."

"Jade, last night was the first time since I moved into my apartment, that I looked forward to going home. It was because I knew you would be there. I knew you had showered there because the place smelled like vanilla. It smelled like heaven. It was wonderful to see that you had made me supper, bought a few groceries, and put a woman's touch on the place. In the morning, it was hard to leave because you were there. I guess, I don't want to miss you at my place, if you decide to leave or if this doesn't work out. I realized last night that I would miss you if and when you left, and it would be hard to go home. For me, its just easier if we stay at the hotel. I need to focus on the case. Do you understand what I'm trying to say?"

Jade could tell he was being cautious again. "I understand Mark. I would probably feel the same way if you were staying at my place. Lets just see where things go. Now, can we concentrate on the here and now?"

"Sure, that sounds like a plan. Actually, I want to tell you about my plan."

"Does it have anything to do with you and I having an incredible night together?" Jade said.

"Oh, most definitely. No rush. Let's finish our wine and when we're done…. he just gave her a mischievous grin while looking at her over his wine glass.

They had started kissing passionately the second the elevator door closed from the lobby to the third floor. They couldn't keep their hands off each other. Once in the hotel room, he broke the kiss even though they were both breathing heavy.

"Mark are you okay?" Jade asked puzzled.

He just looked at her. "Jade, I don't want you to think that our relationship is like two ships passing in the night. I…. I just wanted you to know that I care about you very much. I don't want to hurt you again."

"I know Mark. Ever since the night you told me you were crazy about me."

"I am crazy about you. Believe it Jade."

Once in the room, he was kissing her with sensual pleasure. She removed his shirt and unbuttoned his pants.

Jade couldn't help but stare at him. His chest and arms were muscular, and his six-pack was a sight. His dark chest hair was thick and thinned on the way down to his abdomen, hiding below the waist band of his pants. They both stepped closer to each other and undressed each other. All she had to do was look at his eyes to know what he wanted. She took her time pleasing him with her mouth and tongue. His erection could not be ignored. He touched her face and gently moved her away from his shaft. She came up to look at him. He cupped her face with both hands and began kissing her. He took her hand and led her to the bed.

"Get on your hands and knees honey and lets have some fun." She brought her head lower to the pillow, exposing more of her moist warm sex and curls. He touched her, and she cried out. He covered his shaft with a condom and penetrated her from behind, moving in and out, filling her with pure pleasure.

He continued to move pleasing her. Then he stopped and separated himself from her, gently guided her on to her back, mounted her and penetrated her once again. He was moving faster now.

"Open your eyes Jade and look at me." She did and saw he was looking at her with such warmth and tenderness. She caressed his face. They enjoyed each other for quite some time. He suckled her breasts, flicking her nipples with his tongue, while filling her with his shaft. She found her release, arching her back, and crying out his name. His orgasm followed right after. She could feel him tense up, then his entire body spasmed. After a while, he was still.

All he said was, "you are incredible Jade. I can't get enough of you. You're going to kill me." Then he basically fell on her. She didn't move, rather she was playing with his hair.

"You're not so bad yourself there sweetheart."

They took a shower together then got under the covers and held each other until they fell asleep.

Mark woke up in the middle of the night. Got out of bed, without waking Jade and went to the window, looking out at the darkness. He turned and looked at Jade sleeping soundly. He thought, I almost said it last night. I almost told her that I loved her. If she chooses to leave, it will kill him. He can't stop seeing her though. She's like the air he breathes. He was going to have to tell her and let the chips fall where they may. She will need to make a choice once he tells her.

CHAPTER 21

Ross was at the station before Shapiro. He didn't get much sleep, so he thought, I might as well go to the station and get some work done. He left Jade a note explaining he would call her later. Ross felt in his bones, that the perp who killed Macy also killed Skylar. He also felt that the guy Macy was seen with, in the black sedan, is the killer. He was talking to himself, "this guy has a problem with women having sex for money, or he doesn't like rejection. He's insecure. Maybe he's a religious fanatic who believes prostitutes are evil. Who knows?"

"Is that what you think, he's a religious fanatic? Shapiro asked surprised

"No way. I think this guy killed Macy because she rejected him. Macy pissed him off?

"That's exactly what I think." Shapiro agreed.

"Macy is seen with some john in a black sedan and later disappears and is found dead. That's a hell of a coincidence. Don't you think? Something happened during their encounter. Macy's mouth got her into a lot of trouble most of the time. Maybe this time it got her killed." Ross said.

Shapiro agreed. "I can see it but what about Skylar? Do you think she rejected this guy too?"

"I think she did on some level. Skylar and Macy were from different worlds, but somehow these two cases are connected." Ross answered.

Both Ross and Shapiro looked up to see Ryder Campbell. They met him at the front desk.

"Detectives, I'm in town today on business with your mayor. I thought I'd drop by and give you a sample of my DNA as you requested.

Shapiro had him sign in and escorted him to a private room. The rooms all had cameras. Shapiro grabbed a swab from inside the cabinet in the room and swabbed inside Campbell's cheek for a few seconds. He labelled the container and sent it off to the lab.

"Thank you very much for your cooperation, Mr. Campbell."

"My pleasure. I have nothing to hide. I need to leave, or I will be late."

Shapiro returned to his desk. "I wish all "persons of interest" were as cooperative as Campbell. Now if we can only get Judge Hamilton to give us a DNA sample."

Jade was just heading over to her sister's place to finish cleaning it out when her phone rang. She answered her blue tooth, "hello."

"Jade its Kim, how are you doing? I got your message."

"I'm good. I'm heading to the apartment now. I have Gemma House and the library picking up items that I am donating in Skylar's name."

"Jade, I just can't come over. I would be a complete mess. I hope you understand.

"No, that's fine. I understand. Is there anything you would like from the apartment? It will be cleaned out by the end of the weekend, and I'll be giving the keys back to the management company on Monday."

"I would like the pictures of her and I if that's okay with you. There is also a tote bag on the back of her bedroom door, which says "free spirit" on it with a cartoon of a woman on a motorcycle. She loved that bag. It was her and it would always remind me of her."

Jade thought, that's true. Her sister was always a free spirit. Always did what she wanted to do. "Sure Kim, that's no problem. Come by the hotel this afternoon to pick everything up."

"I'll be there about three p.m."

Jade watched as the truck from Gemma House picked up the furniture and the library van picked up all the books. It was bittersweet to watch, but it had to be done. Skylar was never coming back to her. She was never going to hear her voice again or see her smile. She was never going to have nieces or nephews or grow old with her. Jade missed her sister. She went back in and packed the clothes she was going to donate to the women's centre. She had rented a van from Enterprise just for the day. She packed everything she would donate and also packed the items Kim had requested. She had already packed and removed the items she wanted yesterday.

Jade was walking out to the street with the last box, to the van. There was no where else to park it. She notice a white Lexus stop, with two gentlemen in it. It stopped behind her van and Dr. Martins got out and walked over.

"Hello Dr. Martins." Jade said.

"I thought it was you. Dr. Sinclair and I were just heading back to the hospital from lunch. Can I help you with that box?"

"No but thank you. I'm done." She noticed Dr. Sinclair wouldn't even look at her, when she looked over at him, sitting in the car. He kept looking away. "I just finished packing up the last of my sister's belongings."

"You did that alone? Why didn't you call someone? I would have been more than happy to help. What about Kim?"

"I didn't ask for help, Dr. Martins. It was something I had to do myself. I needed some type of closure, but I thank you for the offer. Kim couldn't deal with coming back here."

"Well, I see your busy, so I'll let you get to it. You take care of yourself, Jade. Perhaps, once your done with your sister's affairs, we could finish that date, we didn't get a chance to finish."

"I'm afraid not, Dr. Martins. I will probably be going back to the Sault. I need to get back to work. I was seriously giving some thought to staying here, but I just don't know. Thank you for your kindness, Dr. Martins."

It was closer to two-thirty by the time she got back to the Enterprise parking lot to return the van. She transferred the packed items for Kim, into her vehicle and went back to the hotel. Kim was driving into the parking lot as Jade was getting out of her car. "Hey Kim."

"Hey yourself." Kim came over and gave her a big hug. "How are you doing?"

"I'm okay. I have my moments but cleaning out her apartment has giving me some kind of closure. I am letting my lawyer manage the financial part of it, so that relieves some of the stress. I packed the stuff you wanted. Its all in this box, including the tote bag."

"Thank you. I just couldn't do it. I would have broken down for sure. Your strong Jade."

"Its amazing the strength you find when you need to. Do you want to go to the hotel restaurant and have a bite? I missed lunch."

"No, I need to go home and relax. I worked last night and haven't gone to bed because I am off tonight, so I typically don't sleep during the day, or I won't sleep at night. My body is all screwed up. Thanks for letting me keep some of Skylar's stuff."

"I'm sure she would have wanted you to have it. Go rest now."

"Take care Jade. Call me."

Jade knew that Kim wouldn't call her. She was hurting right now. She had never experienced the death of a loved one, until now. In time her life would go on to something new. She was young and although she would never forget Skylar, she would move on. Jade thought, in her thirty-two years, she had lost her parents and he sister. She had experienced enough loss for a lifetime.

Ross was thinking of Jade, while sitting at his desk. He thought about what he almost said last night.

"What's on your mind? You look deep in thought. You look like a man in love."

Ross then lifted his head and looked at Shapiro. "In love! What are you talking about? We've only known each other a little less than a month."

"Its not about time, my friend but rather how you feel about her. I fell in love with my wife Anita, during our first date. I knew I was going to marry her." Shapiro shared.

"How did you know you were going to marry her?"

"I can't explain it. Its how I felt about her. I just knew she was the one for me. It sounds strange, but its true."

"How long have you been married now?" Ross asked.

"Almost twenty-five years. The best twenty-five years of my life. I'm going to give you a piece of advice Mark.

If you love this girl, then tell her before someone else does and she's gone from your life forever. Don't be a fuckin idiot." Shapiro smiled.

It was almost four o'clock and there was nothing new on the Skylar Rose case. Both Ross and Shapiro were becoming discouraged. They didn't want this case to end up in a cold case box. They wanted it solved. They had spoken to numerous people, contacted other police agencies to determine if there were any unsolved murders that had similarities to this case, collected evidence and still nothing they can use, right now.

Shapiro and Ross were mulling over evidence and reports when Ross' phone rang. Looking at the caller ID, it was Dr. Lind.

"Give me some good news, Doc."

"Detective Ross, toxicology report came back for Macy Collins, and she had minute traces of chloroform in her blood. Same as Skylar Rose. The trace evidence we found came from the alley itself. Nothing new. No further biological evidence was found except the semen on her hands. I'm still waiting for results. There were no fingerprints either, just like the Skylar Rose case. The dress she was wearing yielded nothing except trace that was present in the alley way itself. Once again nothing new. Let's hope that the semen, tells us something. Otherwise, we have nothing to connect the two cases and we have nothing to help us solve this murder."

Jade was sitting in her hotel room, surfing the net for employment opportunities in Sudbury, when her phone rang. "Hello"

"May I please speak to Jade Rose, please?"

"This is Jade."

"Ms. Rose, my name is Cam Tanner. I received your resume here at the college for the position of full-time Culinary Chef Instructor. Your resume is very impressive. Would you be willing to come in for an interview on Monday morning at ten a.m.?"

"That would be wonderful, Mrs. Tanner! I look forward to meeting you Monday. Thank you."

"Wonderful, Ms. Rose, have a great weekend."

Jade was excited. She thought, no late nights at a restaurant or working every weekend. Even though she enjoyed working in restaurants, it was hard on a relationship. You never had time for a relationship. She wanted something more solid in her life. She wanted normal working hours. She wanted to settle down and maybe have a family. She wondered if Mark wanted kids.

CHAPTER 22

Jade arrived early for her interview. She was dressed in a navy-blue polo dress and white canvas slip on shoes. She was wearing little make-up and let her long hair just flow. She hadn't slept at all. Her and Mark had spent the weekend together, laughing, talking, and making love. She knew they were having more than just sex. She was surprised to hear, he wanted to get married some day and have kids, if it was in the cards. She thought, he was a great guy. They had a lot in common besides the sex. Neither one of them had any family left. It was like two lost souls finding each other.

Jade's thoughts were interrupted when she heard her name, "Ms. Rose, I'm Cam Tanner. Please follow me to my office."

Cam Tanner was of average height but very attractive. She had beautiful green eyes with auburn shoulder length hair. Her office was nicely decorated in light colors of blue and yellows. She had degrees and accomplishments hung on the wall behind her desk. And of course, the shelves were full of culinary books.

"Please have a seat Jade, may I call you Jade?"

"Thank you and yes, please call me Jade."

Jade flew through the interview. It was one of the best interviews she had ever had. Mrs. Tanner was easy going and not stuffy. During the interview, she asked Jade to call her Cam. Mrs. Tanner, she said was her mother-in-law. Jade found out she also studied at the Cordon Bleu in Ottawa. They talked about professors they both had and reminisced about their experiences.

"Well Jade, I think you're perfect for this position. I've interviewed quite a few people for this position, but didn't get the feeling, I get with you. I am offering you the job. All that I need now is to check your references, but I'm sure they will be fine. The position doesn't start until the new school year in September. Will that work for you?"

"That will be fine! It will give me time to move to Sudbury. Thank you so much."

"It was a pleasure meeting you, Jade. I should know by the end of the day if your references check out. If they do, I will ask you to come in to sign a contract detailing the offer of employment and salary."

"It was a pleasure meeting you as well, Cam. I look forward to your call. Thanks again."

Jade was so excited. Finally, she thought, things are starting to work out. She knew her references would check out. She felt bad for leaving the Longos. They had been so good to her, but she needed to move on. She should have done this along time ago, maybe things would have been different for her and Skylar.

She spent the afternoon looking at perspective apartments on the internet. She was jumping the gun. She was being hopeful. She wondered, if she did get the job, how would Mark feel about her staying permanently. Would it scare him off because now it's a reality or would he embrace it? She said out loud, "well she's going to find out one way or another, when she tells him." First, she'll wait for the phone call confirming she got the job.

Shapiro had just gotten off the phone with the lab. "The DNA results from the semen found on Macy's hands matched the pubic hair found on Skylar Rose."

"The same bastard killed both victims." Ross said. "We have a connection, thanks to Macy. Now we just have to catch the bastard, and we will."

Shapiro and Ross wanted to share the news with Moore and Gladstone. "If you need our assistance, let us know." Gladstone said.

It was almost three o'clock and Shapiro and Ross were working on reports and logging evidence that should have been done prior.

Ross' phone rang. He looked at the caller ID but didn't recognize the number., "Detective Ross."

"Detective this is Judge Hamilton. Would you be able to meet me at my office? I would like to give you my DNA sample. I will not come there to do it, for obvious reasons. I don't need people asking why I am there."

"Judge Hamilton, in order to obtain a sample, I will need my partner with me as part of the record. I hope you understand."

"That's fine. I don't want anyone to know except for you and your partner. Would you be able to come right now?"

"We'll be there in twenty minutes."

Ross told Shapiro about meeting with Judge Hamilton. "I'm going to get a swab right now. Meet you out front." Shapiro said.

Shapiro had obtained the swab from Judge Hamilton by swabbing the inside of his cheek. Both he and Ross could see the Judge was feeling compassionate empathy for what happened to Skylar a.k.a. Catherine.

"I thought about our last phone call Detective Ross, and I wanted to help, but I had to think about my family and career. Catherine was a lovely person and didn't deserve what happened to her."

"Sometimes our conscience won't let us rest until we do the right thing. That inner voice keeps nagging at you." Shapiro said.

"That's why I called you. I need you to look for her killer and not waste your time on me. She deserves your undivided attention."

"Thank you for your cooperation, Judge Hamilton." Shapiro said. They both left the Judge's chambers.

"Ross, you had a feeling that these two cases were connected, and I have a feeling the connection is in my hand. Although, I don't think the Judge is our killer, I do think he is hiding something. Something that is invaluable to both these cases.

Ross knew that when Shapiro got one of his "feelings," he was never wrong. "Well, then let's put a rush on that sample. Maybe we can get it back before the three days that it usually takes." Now its just a waiting game.

Jade had been jumpy every time her phone rang. This time was no different. The caller ID identified it was the college.

"Hi Jade, its Cam. Well, the job is yours if you're still interested."

"Oh, I'm very interested! Thank you. I have been dreaming of a position like this."

"Wonderful. Drop by my office tomorrow afternoon to sign your contract. The actual position starts mid August."

"I'll be there tomorrow afternoon Cam. Thank you so much! I'll be ready to start anytime. See you tomorrow!"

Jade was so excited to tell Mark. He hadn't called her yet. He must be having a busy day. She really wanted to cook dinner. She was tired of going out.

Her phone rang. "Speak of the devil," she said out loud. "Hey you."

"Hi baby, you sound different." Everything okay Jade?

"I have great news to share with you. I'll tell you when I see you. When am I gong to see you? What are you hungry for Mark?"

He smiled to himself. "That's a loaded question, darling."

"I'm tired of eating out. I would rather cook." Jade said.

"I'm getting tired of eating out too. I'll pick you up and we'll go to my place. I want to tell you something. We can have supper there. Do you need any groceries? Oh, by the way, bring an overnight bag, cause you're not leaving."

"Mark is everything alright? I bought enough groceries last time I was there. I thought we weren't going to your place anymore."

"We need to talk. I'll be there in an hour."

There's the slut with her bag, waiting at the front door of the hotel. Where is she staying tonight, or should I say "who is she screwing tonight" because it certainly wasn't him. Not tonight anyway, but soon. He was getting hard just thinking of having his way with Jade. Here comes the man of the hour, Detective Ross. They were probably going back to his place. You have all the fun you want because soon it will be my turn with Jade. All the fun will eventually be coming to an end when I kill her.

Jade had made spaghetti with chicken parmesan for supper. They enjoyed a nice glass of white wine with it as well. Jade could tell Mark had something on his mind. He wanted to talk about something. Jade was afraid to initiate the conversation. She didn't want her heart broken after the kind of day she had. It was a wonderful day.

"Jade, I care about you."

Oh god I can't believe this. He's going to end things, she thought. "What is it, Mark? You care about me but…..... its not going to work so why go on with this? Is that what your trying to tell me because you hardly said two words during dinner."

"What the hell are you talking about Jade? No that's not what I'm trying to say. This is coming out all wrong."

"Why don't you just say, what you want to say Mark." Jade asked softly.

Mark looked at Jade. "I love you, Jade. I've loved you since the first time we had dinner at the hotel. I wanted to tell you last night, but I couldn't. I don't want you to leave. I want you to move to Sudbury and move in with me. We can get a bigger place if you want. I don't care as long as you're with me."

Jade had tears in her eyes. Mark looked at her thinking she was going to leave. She was emotional because she doesn't want to hurt him.

"I love you too, Mark. I don't want to go. I want to stay with you. That's part of the good news I wanted to tell you about. I've been looking for a job and I found one.

I've taken a full-time position at the college as a Culinary Chef Instructor. I sign my contract tomorrow. I'm not going anywhere except where you are."

He walked over to her side of the table and kissed her. She kissed him back. They just looked at each other for a while. "Is this what you meant when you said you were working on something.?

"Yes, I didn't want to tell you right away because I didn't know how you would feel. It's real now. I thought it would be best to keep it to myself, until something panned out."

"I don't want to talk about any plans tonight, Jade. We can talk about where we are going to live tomorrow. Tonight, I just want to make love to you. That's all."

They had a beautiful night of passionate love making. In the morning, Ross called Shapiro and told him he wouldn't be in till later around eleven o'clock. He just wanted to stay with Jade a little longer. He was going to take a shower and invited her to take one with him.

"Come take a shower with me, Jade"

"He turned on the water to a comfortable temperature. "Is this okay for you.?"

"Its perfect and she got in. She put her head under the shower head. She tilted her head back causing her breasts to lift.

Mark got into the shower and took her all in. She was a sight. He moved closer to her, caressed her face with both hands and kissed her passionately. She opened her mouth to him, and his tongue danced with hers. His hands were caressing her breasts gently, as he suckled her nipples. Jade had her arms around his neck and arched her back to give him more access. His hands then moved down to her beautiful ass. He just loved the curve and shape of her ass. He touched her moist, warm area and she moaned. She wrapped one hand gently around his shaft, moving up and down his length. This caused him to groan. They were staring at each other with lust in their eyes, while water was coming down on both of them.

"Want to lather me up, Mark?"

Mark added soap to her sponge and then lathered her up. She was full of soap and then she used the sponge on him. Soap made it easier to move her hand along his shaft. His hand returned to her sex, rubbing, and touching her gently, while the other wrapped around her waist, holding her close and steady.

He could feel Jade was unraveling and continued to rub her moist area, while kissing her. Her orgasm sent her over the edge, and she cried out in ecstasy. "That's my girl." Mark smiled.

She smiled back at him and said, "now your turn darling." Jade continued to move her soapy hand up and down his shaft, touching the sensitive tip. He groaned and his release followed, grinding into her while holding her. Once they were finished, they both lathered and washed each other, without getting involved again.

CHAPTER 23

ROSS WALKED INTO THE STATION and was in a great mood. While he was at work, Jade was looking for an apartment for both of them to live in. He couldn't believe what was happening with him and Jade. He was happy.

"Good morning, Shapiro. How are things.?"

"Well, good morning, Detective Ross, how are you doing this morning? You look like all is good in your world."

"We'll talk later. Anything new with the case?"

"DNA results came back with no match to Ryder Campbell. There was no match to the semen or pubic hair. Another dead end. We're running out of leads." Shapiro said. "I still think Judge Hamilton is the key to this case and he doesn't even now it."

"What does that mean? How could he be the key and not know it?" Ross was puzzled.

"Ross hear me out. Skylar a.k.a. Catherine is seen at the Windsor Park Hotel and every time she leaves, there is a black sedan that follows her. Who is she there to see?

Judge Hamilton. There's no black sedan at the Savoy Hotel waiting for her after she sees Ryder Campbell. I'm telling you this has to do with Judge Hamilton somehow and Skylar got caught in the crossfire. That's what my gut tells me. I'm still digging into the Judge's past but like I said before, it's proving to be difficult. He is hiding something. I just know it."

"Do you think Judge Hamilton feels guilty for Skylar's death because he knows who the killer is and is he protecting this sociopath? Ross asked.

"I don't know that. I do believe he is connected somehow." Shapiro repeated.

"Detective Ross or Shapiro, there is a Detective Simon Hill on line three for either one of you. He says he's from Toronto Police Services." Officer Tilley explained.

Ross thanked Tilley, while he picked up the line. "This is Detective Ross."

"Detective Ross, this is Detective Simon Hill from the Toronto Police Service."

"What can I do for you Detective Hill?"

"I think we're looking for the same guy. I received an alert from the Major Case Management system. The DNA evidence that you put into the National Canadian DNA bank from your last two murder cases matches the DNA evidence we put into the bank years ago. A University of Toronto medical student, Jordan Lenski was found dead in the Black Creek Parkland Park in February of 2007. She was sexually and physically assaulted. Coroner said, she was stabbed to death. Two stab wounds to the abdomen. She bled out. The park was a secondary murder scene. She wasn't killed there. There was no evidence. No digital or trace evidence. There were no fingerprints. No fibres or footprints. It was like she was just dropped there from the air. The one thing that was found was a pubic hair. Just like your first case. We interviewed her friends and family. According to them, she was a real sweetheart and had no enemies. Professors were interviewed and they said the same thing. She was a bright student. She had disappeared for three days before she was found in the park and had been dead for approximately six hours when she was found. The last person to see her alive was her date, Mike Mullins. He was interviewed at great length. Volunteered his DNA and he wasn't a match. Further, he was part of the U of T (University of Toronto) hockey team and the next morning he left with the rest of the team to play in London and then Windsor. He was cleared as a suspect. Until now, we've had zilch on this case. After Jordan's murder, her mother would come in at least once a week to inquire, then as time passed, she would come in less. She still comes in once a year. I would love to tell her that her daughter's killer has been caught and will pay for what he did. This case has haunted me for the last fifteen years. Before I die or retire, whichever comes first, I need to find this bastard."

Detective Hill sounded and spoke like a veteran detective. He knew the case of Jordan Lenski inside out.

He probably ate, slept, and made love to, the case. He wanted to catch this bastard.

"Hill, we find anything, we'll let you know." Ross reassured him.

"Thanks Ross. Let's stay in touch."

Ross told Shapiro everything Detective Hill said. "This psychopath has killed three women that we know of. Then we're dealing with a serial killer." Shapiro said. "This guy is really pissing me off."

Mark drove Jade back to the hotel to pick up her car. She had a few things to take care of. At noon she was having lunch in a local dinner where she set up two appointments to view potential apartments in the afternoon. She was watching the news while eating. The female anchor was reporting on the murder of a local prostitute.

"Police are still looking into the murder of nineteen-year-old, Macy Collins. She was found dead two days ago in an alley way under the Bridge of Nations. She had disappeared five days ago. Her roommate reported her missing when she didn't come home. Police are not saying how or when she died. Ms. Collins was well known to the police. If anyone has any information about this case, please call the Sudbury Police Services. This is Kelly Belmar, with Northern Ontario, Channel 10 News."

Jade thought, that poor girl. She wondered if her sister's murder was connected to this young girl's murder. She knew Mark couldn't and wouldn't tell her. Jade needed to leave so she wanted to pay for her lunch. She opened her wallet, and a photo of Skylar was looking back at her from within a plastic insert. Jade touched the photo lightly with the tip of her index finger.

"How I miss you little sister." She said to herself. Then she heard a voice asking her if she was okay. It brought her back to what she was doing. Jade looked up to see the waitress.

"Are you ready for the bill dear?"

"Yes, thank you."

After lunch, Jade had gone to see the first apartment and didn't care for it. The building wasn't kept up, she could hear noise coming from other apartments, and the apartment itself was small. She had time before she had to go see the second apartment, so she decided to go to the college to sign her contract.

Jade felt so relieved now that the contract was signed. "Now its official," she said. She was also very pleased with her salary and benefits. She had a half hour to get to the south end of the city. She was going to look at an apartment overlooking Ramsey Lake. The building and grounds were well maintained. The apartment was beautiful, with hardwood floors and views of the lake from every window and two large bedrooms. It had plenty of storage and every floor had laundry facilities. It was actually perfect for her and Mark.

"The unit is beautiful. I would like to talk to my partner about it. What is the rent worth and when is it available?" Jade asked the superintendent.

Ms. Sawyer, the superintendent explained, "the rent is $2100 per month, which includes utilities and there is a one-year lease. I would need first and last month's rent prior to you moving in. The unit will be available September 1. It needs to be cleaned, painted and this unit is due for new appliances, kitchen cabinets and counters."

"That's wonderful. How long do I have to give you an answer?"

"Ms. Rose, I will give you twenty-four hours, and then I have to keep showing it"

"That's fair Ms. Sawyer. I will let you know tomorrow by noon, then."

Ms. Sawyer gave her an application that was the standard and it included a section for references as well.

"Thank you. Talk to you tomorrow."

Jade was really excited to talk to Mark about the apartment. She couldn't wait to see him. She was going back to the hotel to pick up the last of her belongings and to check out.

He couldn't figure out what she was doing. She's sleeping with him but has gone to two other apartment buildings. Is there someone else at the college? This slut sure gets around. Now she's leaving the hotel with two suitcases and a box. Is she leaving town? I hope not. That would ruin all his plans. Then it dawned on him. She is moving in with him, while screwing the others she has on the go. Nothing but a slut like her sister. She is moving in with him and she hardly knows him. He became very angry, "I am going to take my time with you, bitch."

She checked out of the hotel and finally got everything back to Mark's apartment. She kept the box in her car and brought up only the two suitcases. She didn't want to takeover his place. There was so much to do, she thought. First things first, she needed to give her two months notice to her landlord at the end of this month, so she put a reminder into her cell phone. Depending on what Mark had to say about this potential apartment, she was going to have to figure out what to do with her furniture. That was still some time away, she thought. More importantly right now, what was she going to make for dinner tonight? Mark was going to be home in an hour and a half.

Mark got home and had a big smile on his face. "It's great to come home to you, baby." He kissed and hugged her. "Something smells great."

"I made chicken alfredo pasta for supper."

"Let me get changed and wash up and we can eat. How was your day? Did you sign your contract?" When he walked into the bedroom, he noticed her suitcases. He smiled. "So, you've officially moved in. No more hotel."

"Mark, I don't want to takeover your place. If the suitcases bother you, tell me and I'll figure something out."

"Are you kidding, I was happy to see them. So, how was your day. Was it productive?"

"This morning I did a final inspection of Skylar's place and brought the keys back to the management company. So, that's all done, even though bittersweet.

"That must have been tough, Jade. I wish you had waited for me."

"I needed to do it alone, Mark. She was my little sister. It helped me find some closure. On a happier note, I did sign my contract, and may have found us an apartment. Its beautiful and overlooks Ramsey Lake. The rent is comparable, and utilities are included. It will be ready September 1st."

"Jade, do you like the apartment?"

"Yes, I love it."

"Then, I love it too." He just smiled at her. "As long as you're happy, then I'm happy."

"I love you Mark Ross. You are a good man."

They sat down to dinner and talked about future plans. Life was good!

CHAPTER 24

ROSS AND SHAPIRO HAD BEEN at work for hours. They were going over all the evidence they had accumulated, along with witness statements, and autopsy reports to ensure they hadn't missed anything. They knew that none of the three women murdered knew each other, but there was a common denominator. They just needed to find it. "We're still waiting on DNA results from Judge Hamilton." Shapiro said.

"Those results should be in today or tomorrow. I can tell you're anxious. You just can't wait to see those results." Ross noticed about Shapiro.

"Ross, I don't want this case to haunt me for the rest of my fuckin life. Every cop fears there's always one case that lives with them, if its not solved. We need to find justice for these women. We need to find justice for their families. They need closure. This will be that case for me. I don't sleep now because I keep going over and over things in my mind."

"I understand exactly what you mean. I need to tell Jade that we found her sister's killer, or I'm afraid she will never be whole. I told her how I felt. I told her that I loved her." Ross confessed.

"Finally. Good man. And…... don't stop there. How do you feel? What did she say?" Shapiro said.

"She loves me too. I feel great. I'm a very lucky man. I could have lost her the way I was acting. A very smart man told me not to be a fuckin idiot." Ross laughed.

"So, what now? Is she moving here?"

"She is and she's already secured a job at the college. We are moving in together." Ross was happy to say.

"I wish you all the best my friend. Don't screw this up or I'll kill you. I like her. She's good for you."

Ross was going to say something, but Shapiro's phone rang. Looking at caller ID, it was Dr. Lind. "Dr. Lind what can I do for you?"

"Detective Shapiro, I have the results for Judge Hamilton's DNA test. Would you and Detective Ross come down to my office?"

"Sure, we'll be there in fifteen minutes." Shapiro said.

Shapiro told Ross Dr. Lind wanted to see them. "Why does he need to see us, rather than just tell us about the results over the phone?"

"I guess we're going to find out, but this could be the break we're looking for. At least I hope so." Shapiro was anxious.

Even though it wasn't Dr. Lind who conducted the testing on the DNA, he was the one that spoke for the DNA specialist. They were all forensic scientist trying to solve murders. Ross and Shapiro arrived in ten minutes and went right to Dr. Lind's office.

"Good afternoon gentlemen. I called you here to explain the results of this particular DNA sample. Judge Hamilton is not the person you are looking for. His DNA sample does not match the pubic hair or semen found on the murder victims."

"Why couldn't you just tell us that over the phone Dr. Lind, rather than us having to high tail it here?" Shapiro was annoyed.

"Although, the sample does not match Judge Hamilton, there are several DNA markers that do."

"What the hell does that mean, Doc?" Ross was frustrated.

"As you both of you know, the DNA Identification Act, which introduced the National DNA Data Bank prohibits familial DNA testing in Canada due to privacy issues. Because of this we look at genetic markers."

"Doc, what are you getting at? What does all this mean?" Ross said again.

"It could mean that the killer is related to Judge Hamilton. We are running more tests to determine if we can find more genetic markers. If there are more, the probability is that it is a son or brother. The Judge's father is deceased, I presume."

"So, let me get this straight," Shapiro said. "Judge Hamilton is not the killer, but a son or brother is or could be?"

"That's correct Detective Shapiro. While we are running the testing for more genetic markers, I suggest you find out if the Judge has a son or brother. It may come down to that." Dr. Lind explained.

"We know he has a son. But the son was with him at the daughter's wedding. We have pictures, receipts, and witness statements. We're going to need a DNA sample from the son to rule him out. That's going to go over like a fart in church, asking the Judge for a sample of his son's DNA." Ross pointed out.

"Doc, can you run a paternity test on the Judge's sample with the pubic hair and semen found on the murder victims? Won't the paternity test tell us conclusively if it is the son?" Shapiro asked.

"I can have the lab do that, and the test will confirm if it is the son. It will take a couple of days or maybe longer."

"The Judge is starting to piss me off. I want the DNA sample from the son, and I want the god damn truth, cause he is hiding something. I don't give a shit if he's a Judge. I'm tired of tippy toeing around the Judge because of who he is. Let's go see him now." Shapiro was mad.

Ross and Shapiro drove to the Court House. They had no appointment or idea if the Judge was free, and they really didn't care. They went directly to the Judge's chambers, but first needed to get by the Judge's assistant, who was sitting behind his desk int the reception area.

"Gentleman, I don't believe you have an appointment with Judge Hamilton today."

"You tell the Judge we need to meet with him and we're not leaving until we see him today." Ross demanded.

"He is in court right now and will be there for the next half hour."

"We'll wait. We're not going anywhere." Shapiro said firmly.

Jade had sent an email to her landlord explaining that as of the first of the month, she was giving her sixty days notice. She also called Ms. Sawyer to inform her that she and Mark will take the apartment. "I will be bringing you first and last months rent cheques, as well as the application this afternoon. I hope that's okay."

"That's fine dear. I'm glad you took it. When you come in, I will have you sign the rental agreements, regarding certain rules we have in the building."

"Thank you, Ms. Sawyer."

Jade had a few questions for Ms. Sawyer. She wondered, if the apartment could be painted a subtle bluish gray, as it was white now. If an air conditioner could be used during the summer months and how many parking spots were allotted to each apartment.

"I need to get some groceries, while I'm out," she said to herself.

Ross and Shapiro had waited forty-five minutes before Judge Hamilton returned to his chambers.

"Judge Hamilton, Detectives Ross and Shapiro are here to see you and there not leaving until they do. They have been waiting for almost an hour." His assistant explained.

Judge Hamilton wondered what they could want. "Show them in please."

Shapiro walked in first and did without the pleasantries. "Judge Hamilton your DNA sample was not a match to the DNA evidence we have on the murder case of Skylar Rose. But we did discover something interesting though."

"And what would that be?"

"Your sample and the samples we have in evidence, have several genetic markers that match. We are checking them now for more genetic markers."

"Forgive me. Your talking to me like I'm supposed to know what the hell you're talking about. When I don't have a clue."

Shapiro looked him directly in the eye and said, "the markers mean that the killer is related to you. The probability is either a brother or son."

"I don't have a brother and my son was with me during the murder of that young lady. Don't you even think about implicating my son in this mess. He hasn't done anything." He said firmly.

"We need a DNA sample from your son to conclusively rule him out. Unless you have another son somewhere."

The Judge quickly turned his head towards Shapiro and gave him a look of fear. He was just staring at Shapiro. Ross noticed the statement had startled the Judge.

"If your son doesn't provide a DNA sample, we will turn every rock over to get it. I don't care if I have to drag your name out in public, your Honor. I am trying to keep this quiet for the sake of your family, but if I have to, I will obtain a warrant. Whoever is killing has killed three woman and it has to stop." Shapiro was serious.

"Three woman! What are you talking about Detective Shapiro?"

"I'm talking about a serial killer in our city. I can't discuss ongoing investigations. Just be sure, that we won't stop until this person is found. Now about your son's DNA."

While Shapiro was talking and drilling the Judge, Ross stood back and watched his body language. Sometimes what people don't say but reveal on their face or in their body language speaks louder than words. Ross saw genuine concern in the Judge's face.

There was a knock on the door. A young man in his early thirties poked his head in. "Hi dad, you ready to go?

"Detectives Shapiro and Ross, this is my son Milo Hamilton. "Judge Hamilton said proudly. "We were just talking about a case son. I'll be right with you son. Just give us a couple more minutes please."

"Sure, no problem dad. I'll just wait out in the reception area. Milo turned to Ross and Shapiro, "it was nice meeting you both." Milo shut the door and stepped out into the waiting room."

"Gentlemen, I am not saying another word without my lawyer present. I won't be manipulated or harassed, and I won't allow for my family either. Now, please leave my office.

As Ross and Shapiro were leaving, Ross noticed Milo Hamilton drinking from a Styrofoam cup. Once done, he threw the white Styrofoam cup in the garbage near the chair he was sitting in. Milo got up and entered his father's chambers and shut the door. Ross took out a tissue from his coat pocket, retrieved the cup from the bottom using a Kleenex, being very careful not to touch the rim. Ross placed the cup in a plastic bag when he got back to the car.

Ross and Shapiro left the courthouse with what they came for but thought they would never get. Shapiro knew he had the Judge's head spinning. He needed to get Milo Hamilton's DNA back to the lab and put a rush on it.

"Shapiro, do you remember when you said the Judge is hiding something?"

"I remember and I still think he is." Shapiro said.

Ross remembers the look on the Judge's face when Shapiro implied, he had another son somewhere. "You had to see the look on his face when you suggested he had another son somewhere. He had a look on his face that I just can't explain. It was one of confusion and fear. He was scared."

"Maybe I hit a nerve." Shapiro said. "Maybe the Judge and his wife lost a son years ago, and what I said brought up some raw emotion and old memories."

They both got back to the station and sent the Styrofoam cup to the lab after it was logged in as evidence for this case.

"I hope we get a hit with the cup. If Milo is not a match, then we are back to square one." Shapiro was hopeful.

Ross was thinking about it and didn't agree. "Dr. Lind said that the genetic markers suggest a relative. If Milo comes back no match, then we are going to have to work on the Judge's other male relatives."

"Are you forgetting, the Judge and his entire family were in the Dominican for the wedding." Shapiro reminded him.

"We're missing a big piece of the puzzle." Ross said.

They both looked at each other. They knew they had to figure out what that missing piece was or more women would be killed.

It was three p.m. by the time Jade made it over to give Ms. Sawyer first and last months rent cheques and completed application. Ms. Sawyer was quite impressed that one of her tenants was a Sudbury Police Detective. It made her feel safer.

"I hope I. not bothering you at this time Ms. Sawyer."

"No not at all dear. I was just doing some landscaping myself, even though we have professional landscapers that do it. I like gardening. I find it therapeutic."

The landscape was beautiful, Jade thought. "The pink peonies and green Hosta are so colorful and healthy looking." Ms. Sawyer, I was hoping I can ask a couple of questions."

"Sure, we can discuss your questions, while you sign forms. How does that sound?"

"That sounds fine. Thank you."

Jade signed at least ten forms ensuring that tenants adhere to Kentwood Management rules. There were no propane barbeques allowed, the hardwood floors had to be kept up by the tenant, no pets allowed except for service animals, and there was no painting allowed unless the management team approved the paint color. Jade thought, that's why the building is so very well-kept up. Every tenant signed the same forms. She liked that. She liked rules. She was happy to hear she could change the paint color and she was allowed to bring in an air conditioner for those hot months. Unfortunately, there was one parking spot allotted for each apartment but there was visitor's parking, if needed.

She left her future home in great spirits but that was short lived. She stopped short of getting to her car. She had a feeling that she was being watched. The feeling started a couple of days ago. Nonchalantly, looking around, she didn't see anything or anyone out of character. She just couldn't shake this feeling. At first, she thought, it was anxiety due to moving to a new city, into a new home with Mark. She wanted things to work out and was worried. She thought maybe, they were moving to fast. But now, the feeling was starting to scare her. She would go to the grocery store tomorrow. She just wanted to get back to Mark's apartment, lock the door and start dinner. It was already four-thirty p.m.

Jade was happy to back at the apartment. She ensured the lock was engaged on the door. Tortellini in Creamy Rosé Sauce was on the menu tonight. It was inexpensive and easy. She hoped Mark would like it. She heard the door open.

He kissed her. "Hey babe, how are you doing? How was your day?"

"My day was productive. I dropped off the rent cheques and application, cleaned the apartment and emailed the landlord of my building, letting them know that as of the first of the month, I would be giving notice. Meanwhile, I need to get the rest of my belongings down here. I'll work on that later. I still have time."

"How was your day, Mark?"

Mark just eyed Jade. "You know I can't tell you anything about the case babe. All I can tell you is that we are still checking out leads."

"Mark, I didn't ask you how your day was because I want information about my sister's case. I ask because I want to know how your day was. That's all."

"I wish I could tell you that we've caught the bastard, but that hasn't happened yet. I hope it will happen soon. I know you need closure."

Jade didn't want to talk about her sister's murder. She was feeling very emotional and was on the verge of tears. "Mark, go wash up and lets eat. I hope you like tortellini."

"Jade, you know you don't have to cook for me. I didn't ask you to move in with me so you could cook for me everyday."

"Are you nuts? I'm a chef, Mark! I love cooking. That's what I do. I would cook all the time if I could."

He just laughed, forgetting who he was talking to. "You do whatever makes you happy baby. Maybe you should open up an Italian eatery of your own."

Jade was happy that Mark loved the tortellini. He enjoyed it with Italian bread and butter and a glass of red wine. They retired to the living room and watched T.V. Mark could tell Jade had something on her mind.

"Jade are you alright?'

"Sure, I'm good, why do you ask?"

"No, you're not good. You're a million miles away. Tell me what's wrong. Are you having second thoughts about moving in together?"

"Absolutely not. Are you Mark?"

"No, of course not. Then what's wrong and don't tell me you're good?"

"Its probably nothing but for the last couple of days, I've had this feeling that someone has been watching me or following me. It happened again when I was leaving the new apartment building today."

"Did you see anything or anyone out of sorts or suspicious?"

"No nothing. I don't really know anyone in Sudbury. I think its just anxiety about the move, the new job, you. I want things to work out. Maybe, I'm just worried, is all."

"Sweetheart, everything will work out. Don't worry. I'm not going anywhere. Regardless, I want you to be aware of your surroundings and I want to know where you are when you're going out. I'm not trying to be controlling. I just need to know you're safe. That's all."

She nearly saw me at the apartment building today. I ducked quickly. She must have got a feeling that someone was watching her. Well, she was right. I assume the detective and her have found a new place to play house together. Isn't that nice. Soon, it won't matter. I'll have her for myself. I'll be the one playing house with her. I'm going to have her every which way because that's what sluts and tramps want. I'll give her what she wants over and over and over and when I've had enough of this slut, I'll kill her. Time to put my plan in action soon.

CHAPTER 25

MARK WOKE UP BEFORE JADE. He didn't really sleep last night. He couldn't stop thinking about what she said last night. She had a feeling someone was following her. He couldn't do his job and worry about her. He needed to call Shapiro.

"Hey Al, its me. Listen, I won't be in till a little later. I have a situation here."

"What's up Mark? You, okay?"

"I'm fine but I'm worried about Jade. Last night she told me she's been having a feeling for the last couple of days, that she is being followed. I remember Kim Marshall saying the same about Skylar."

"It scared the crap out of me. I don't know what to do, short of locking her in this apartment. I told her that she needs to make sure she makes me aware of her whereabouts."

"Really, that's all you can do. Is there a big need for her to go out? If not, than she can wait till you can go with her."

"This is crazy Al. She really doesn't know anyone here, except for her sister's friends from the hospital and the few people she has met while she's been here. I can count those people on one hand."

"Mark its Thursday. You got personal days left, so take today and tomorrow off and stay with her for the next couple of days. Go away with her. Don't worry about anything here. I don't expect any results to come back this week. I can complete overdue reports. I got it covered."

"Thanks Al. I'll do that. If you need me, call me. If not, I'll see you Monday morning."

Mark called his Captain and asked for two personal days which were granted. He took the time to make Jade a nice breakfast and as soon as she woke up, he was going to serve it to her in bed. He could hear her rustling in bed, calling him. He came in with a breakfast bed tray full of eggs, bacon, toast, home fries, orange juice and of course, coffee with cream.

"What's this Mark? Why aren't you at work?"

"I took two personal days, and this is breakfast in bed. Just for you baby. You deserve it"

"So, you don't have to go into work for the next four days?

"That's right. I'm all yours."

"Mark, why did you decide to take two days off now? Does it have something to do with what I told you yesterday? About the feeling that someone is following me."

"Jade, I'm just worried is all. When did you start getting that feeling?"

Jade thought about it and tried to pin point the exact day. "It started the last day I was at my sister's apartment. Nothing out of the ordinary happened though."

"Do you remember who you talked to that day Jade?"

Jade had to think about it. It was several days ago. "I spoke to Ms. Lipton briefly before I left. She gave me a hug. I also spoke to Kim on the phone. Oh, and I also spoke to Dr. Martins. I was just leaving my sister's apartment and was loading stuff in my car. He and his intern were driving by on their way back to the hospital, from having lunch. He stopped and asked if I needed any help, but I told him I was fine. His intern wouldn't even look at me. That was it. I don't think I talked to anyone else."

"You're right. It doesn't seem like anything out of the ordinary. Just be careful Jade. Like I said, I want to know your whereabouts. That means, I want to know where you are going and who you're with. I know that seems to the extreme, but I don't care. Until this feeling goes away, this is how its going to be. Understand?"

"Yes, I understand. Don't' worry about me. Now, since your off for four days and I don't start my job for a few more weeks, why don't you and I take a trip to the Sault? It'll give me a chance to gauge, what I need to sell. Plus, I'll take you to the Bella Cucina for an authentic Italian dinner, while we're there. Have you ever been to the Sault before?"

"Briefly, for work. Lets pack and leave right away."

He was waiting for her to come downstairs and then he would take her. He saw her and her boyfriend, and they were carrying duffel bags, while laughing and holding hands. They were going somewhere together and would be returning God knows when. He was furious. The detective was supposed to be at work, instead he was with her. No! No! This was not happening. He is ruining all my plans. He was so mad, he was punching the dash of his car, with the side of his fist over and over. I hate her. He needed release and went looking for it.

That night, he went back down to the Bridge of Nations to pick up a prostitute for a couple of hours. He was driving a rental car and not his black sedan. He didn't need the cops on his ass. He needed release. *"I want someone that looks soft and is more lady like, if that's even possible with these whores." He said to himself.* He wasn't going to kill her, just screw her brains out. He spotted a tall blonde. *"Hey, honey you up for some fun for a couple of hours? I got five hundred dollars for you."*

"Sure, thing sweetheart. You're cute."

"Get in then. Let's go to the hotel across the street."

"As long as your paying sweetheart, I'll go anywhere you want."

He gave her the money and had her go pay for the room. He didn't want to be seen by anyone unless absolutely necessary. It was the type of hotel where you pay by the hour. The prostitutes knew it well. *"Lets go in an get started, shall we."* Once in the hotel room, he nudged her to the bed. He needed to remember not to draw attention to himself. He was seen by other whores picking up the blonde.

"So, what do you want baby? I can give you anything you want."

"Oh, I bet you can. Just like you've been giving it to every other john, he thought. I want you to make me forget about this woman that has been a bitch to me. Can you do that?"

The prostitute walked up to him and took his jacket off, then started unbuckling his belt. She undid the button to his pants and began touching him.

"Is that making you forget the bitch?"

She was looking at him. He didn't want her looking at him. She was enjoying this. It wasn't about her, he thought. "Enough of this, get on the bed," he ordered. She complied. He was fully erect now. Before mounting her, he put a condom on his length. He penetrated her slowly. "Oh, that feels so good baby." *He told her to stop talking. He wasn't here for her pleasure, only his release. He enjoyed her for quite a while. This whore can go a long time, he thought.* He could feel her coming apart. He didn't care about her. He wanted to find his own release soon. He could go a long time, so this whore was in for the ride of her life. *You're going to work for your money with me.* She was enjoying herself. He could tell. Well too bad for her. His release finally came with a fury. As he was disposing the used condom, she was getting dressed.

"Where do you think you're going, I paid you for two hours."

She just looked at him. "I thought we were done."

"Well, you thought wrong. I still have an hour left with you or you can give me back half of my money."

She wasn't giving the money back. That was for sure. "Sure sweetheart, whatever you want."

He was getting hard again. *"Go over to the table and bend over," he ordered.* He covered his shaft with a new condom. This time he penetrated her hard from behind, moving fast. She yelped. He kept moving for quite sometime. *"Get on the bed," he told her.* He knew she wanted to leave and was tired, but he didn't care. All he cared about was his release, which came soon after.

"When he was done with her, he looked at her and said, *"clean yourself up and get out whore."* She didn't say anything and quickly got out of there.

Jade and Mark had a great car ride to the Sault. They laughed, talked, and planned. They arrived at Jade's apartment around three p.m. They took their bags out of the car and went up to Jade's apartment.

"Nice place honey. Well, I know our new apartment will look gorgeous by the time you're finished with it."

He notice the urn with her sister's ashes, on top of the fireplace mantel.

"Thanks. I always loved this apartment. I've lived her for the last five years. But I am looking forward to moving in with you. I know I'll love it there too. I'm looking forward to decorating our apartment, making it a home for you and I."

"Your furniture is nicer than mine. I would rather sell mine and keep yours or sell everything and buy everything new."

"Well, that can be expensive. I'll want to keep the furniture that works for us and buy what we need."

"Smart, beautiful, and frugal. I'm a lucky man."

"Well, Mr. lucky man, do you want to wash up and get ready to go out for dinner?"

"As long as we can come back here for dessert?"

She smiled at him, walked over, and kissed him tenderly. He returned the kiss. "Sounds like a plan to me." Jade whispered in his ear.

Shapiro had an hour left before his day was over. He had gotten quite a bit of paperwork done. He received a phone call from Detective Simon Hill from Toronto Police Services asking if there was anything new in their cases. Shapiro explained they were working on a lead involving DNA genetic markers.

"Sounds like the lead could be viable. Hopefully, something pans out." Hill said.

"I understand your frustration, I'm feeling it too and our cases aren't as old as yours. With all the modern technology out there, you would figure that something would give, but we keep turning up dead ends. We're running out of leads."

"I know what you're saying Shapiro. Regardless of technology, police work still requires walking the beat and finding the evidence for this modern technology to find the miniscule piece that is needed to put away these bastards."

"So true. We find anything Hill, we'll contact you. No doubt." Shapiro hung up.

Shapiro was thinking, that's all we need is that miniscule piece of evidence to find this asshole. Its like finding a needle in a haystack.

Shapiro's thoughts were interrupted when Officer Tilley dropped an envelope on his desk. "You got mail Detective Shapiro."

Shapiro saw it was from the Office of the Registrar of Ontario. "Are you sure this is for me Tilley?"

"It has your name on it."

He remembers sending out emails and making phone calls when working on the background checks for Judge Hamilton and Ryder Campbell. He opened the envelope and read the letter. "Holy shit" he said out loud. Others in the squad room looked over briefly. Judge Hamilton was married before in 1982 and divorced a year later.

Shapiro wondered if the Judge had any children with his first wife.

There was no further information about the woman he married and divorced. He was going to keep this information in the vault. The information could be valuable at a later time. "I wonder what other surprises the Judge was keeping to himself." Shapiro thought. He would tell Ross about it when he got back Monday morning.

Jade and Mark had spent about three hours at the Bella Cucina Restaurant. Jade introduced him to the Longos, and they all sat, talked and of course, ate. The Longos couldn't say enough about Jade. They loved her like a daughter.

"We only want the best for her," Domenica said. "She will be an excellent instructor. The college is lucky to have her."

Jade thought, she would miss them too. When it was time to leave, she said her good byes. There were hugs and kisses.

"You make sure, you come back and see us Jade and bring your friend, of course. Don't forget about us." Paolo Longo said.

"I'll be back, I promise. How can I forget you? Both of you have been like parents to me. I will miss you."

Jade and Mark finally got back to Jade's place around eight-thirty p.m. Mark had been looking at her all night.

She had people that cared about her here. She felt safe. She laughed and joked like she didn't have a care in the world. He hoped she would feel the same way in Sudbury.

"Those are very special people, The Longos." He said.

"They have always treated me with respect and like one of the family. If it weren't for them, I would have spent many Christmas' alone. Jade worked most holidays."

"You didn't feel scared, today, did you?"

"No, I didn't but I think that has much to do with the fact that you are with me.

"Jade, I want you to feel safe all the time. I hope you can find that sense of security in Sudbury, that you feel here."

She walked over to where he was and touched his face. "I will. Don't worry. Things are just new for me in Sudbury right now. Eventually, I will feel safer. I don't want to stay here anymore. Like I said before, I need a change and I think Sudbury will be a good one."

"You're a tough cookie. Most people in your position, would just stay put and love the family they have, even if they don't share the same blood. Not you. You're diving in head first into unchartered territory."

"There's more than one type of family and you're my family now. That's the way I look at it"

"I love you, Jade. I don't think I've loved you more than I do right now." He looked at her and kissed her passionately. He was going to make love to her tonight.

She wrapped her arms around his neck and kissed him back. They kissed for a long time it seemed. Both, devouring each other.

Without breaking the kiss, they walked back to the bedroom. She broke the kiss, to turn on a lamp to add some ambiance. She wanted to see his face.

"Jade, I want to take my time with you. Do you understand?"

She just nodded in agreement. She slowly undid every button on her shirt. She left it open for Mark to do what he wished. Then she undid the zipper to her jeans. He could see she was wearing matching lace bra and panty. He slowly took off her shirt while kissing her shoulders. His hands were on her shoulders when he took her lips again passionately. He ended the kiss and looked at her. He couldn't take his eyes off of her.

"Let me love you, Jade." He continued to kiss her. He walked her backwards to the bed, undressed her and gently laid her on the bed. He undressed quickly without looking away from her face. His focus at this moment was Jade, and only Jade.

"I need you, Mark."

He covered his shaft with a condom. She began touching herself while looking at him, and this drove Mark crazy. He gently parted her legs, and brought his head down to her moist curls, telling her to continue to touch herself. Jade was in heaven. Then he mounted her and gently penetrated her, filling her slowly. He continued to move in and out. He wanted to enjoy her. She was moaning with pleasure. "I'm not stopping until we both orgasm, Jade." He was moving faster now. Their bodies were in sync with each other. Her beautiful blue eyes were closed. Her body glistened with moisture and her hair was everywhere. She was the epitome of sexy, he thought.

"Look at me baby, look at me. Open your eyes. Look at me while we orgasm together." She opened her eyes and touched his face. It didn't take long until she became unraveled. She arched her back, while crying out his name. He could feel her muscles contract and relax. That caused his release. His entire body spasmed. A few minutes later when he calmed, he looked at her, "that was great honey."

"Mark make love to me again. This time, I'm going to love you." She said.

"No problem baby. Just let me rest a minute."

CHAPTER 26

Ross got up to shower for work. He and Jade had gotten in last evening around seven o'clock. They had a great weekend together. He got to know her better and saw her interacting with people she had known for years. They loved her. He loved her. He didn't want to leave her today, but life gets in the way. He needed to get back to work. Shapiro would have to catch him up on anything new. He wondered if there was anything new. This case is moving at a snail's pace, he thought.

Jade was in the kitchen, pouring herself a cup of coffee, leaning against the counter, when Mark came out of the bathroom.

He went to her and kissed her cheek. "Good morning baby."

"Morning honey."

"What's on your agenda today, Jade? Where are you heading to?"

"Sounds like the third degree."

"No honey. Like I told you before, I want to know where your going and who you're going to see."

"I know Mark. I'm just not use to giving someone a play by play of my day. Anyway, I need to purchase a chef's apron and coat for work. I noticed a uniform shop on Lasalle a while back, so that's where I'm going some time, this morning. I have no plans this afternoon. Maybe go and pick out paint colors for the apartment unless you want to come along. I can wait."

"No thank you, decorating is your department, as long as it's not frilly. I don't like frilly. I'm not trying to be a pain in the ass, I just need to know you're safe. That's all.

Jade was laughing. "Frilly, you're funny. Don't worry, I'll let you know where I'm going today."

"I've got to go Jade. I'm going to be late. Love you." He kissed her cheek and left, ensuring the door was locked.

Ross got to the station around ten a.m. Shapiro was at his desk.

"Hey how was your weekend? How is Jade?

"The weekend was exactly what we needed. Thanks for the suggestion. Jade is fine. I could tell she was more relaxed while we were in the Sault. I told her this morning before leaving, she needs to let me know where she is going."

"I can tell you're worried. I would be worried too, if my wife told me she had a feeling someone was following her."

"She knows I have a job to do. How was your weekend Shapiro?

"Just relaxed mostly. I finally painted the guest bedroom, while Anita was gardening."

"Glad to hear you had a productive weekend. So, anything new on the case partner?"

"Found out Judge Hamilton was previously married."

"Really! When? Who was he married to? For how long?" Ross asked.

"He was married in 1982 and divorced a year later. I don't know who he was married to. That's still a mystery. I'm not going to ask him about his previous marriage. It really has no bearing on the case, as far as I can determine, at this point."

"Interesting. I wonder what other secrets Judge Hamilton is keeping."

"I was wondering that myself after I found out about this marriage. The DNA testing on Milo Hamilton's sample should be back today or tomorrow. Depending on what the results are, we need to keep pressuring Judge Hamilton."

"We need to tread carefully, Shapiro. The man is powerful and could cause problems for us and the department."

"I know, that's why we can't just go barging into his office. We need conclusive proof." Ross reminded him.

"You're right, I get it. But we do have an ace in the hole. His previous marriage. I don't think anyone knows he's been married before. I don't think his wife and family know. I think this is part of what he is hiding. I just don't know why."

"Milo Hamilton is his real son, not adopted. We know that. If he were adopted this would give us nothing as far as the DNA sample."

"No, I checked all that. I've obtained all the birth records for the Hamilton children. Milo Hamilton was born to Theodore and Claire Hamilton in 1990, in Sudbury. He is the eldest of three children born to the couple." Shapiro said.

"If the DNA sample matches, then we have our killer. If not, and the genetic markers continue to match, then we have a problem. Hopefully, the paternity test can tell us something. These tests better come back soon. This asshole has killed two women in the last month. He's bound to kill again." Ross pointed out.

"Somehow Jordan Lenski, Skylar Rose and Macy Collins have crossed paths with this bastard, and it cost them their lives. I want him so bad." Shapiro said.

"You and me, both." Ross agreed.

It was one p.m. and Jade was going to the uniform place on Lasalle. She called Mark to let him know she was heading there right now and once she was done at the uniform shop; she was going to the paint store to look at swatches. She needed to find a light and airy paint color for the apartment. She needed to give the paint swatch to

Ms. Sawyer for approval. She was looking at light blue gray and light taupe. She wanted to bring variations of these colors home and talk to Mark about it. She thought, he's just going to tell her to pick the color she wanted. As soon as she got outside, she got that feeling again. Mark's apartment building didn't have cameras on the outside of the building. She was tired of this feeling.

"Who the hell would be following her?"

Jade got into her car and drove to the uniform shop. She was checking her rear-view mirror but didn't notice anything out of the ordinary. She arrived at the uniform shop and parked her car. She didn't get out right away, but rather surveyed her surroundings. She put to memory what she saw and went into the store. About forty-five minutes later, she came out with a new chef coat and apron. Well, she thought, now I'm off to the paint store. She was looking forward to looking at paint swatches. She got into her car and looked around. Once again there was nothing out of the ordinary. She called Mark to let him know she was on her way to the paint store from the uniform shop. She got to the paint store and was walking to the door.

"The feeling is gone." She said to herself. "Am I losing my mind? I must be stressed."

She spent at least an hour in the paint store. It was like a kid in the candy store. She had picked out two colors. One was a light blue gray called topsail and the other was a light French gray. She wanted to use both colors.

Hopefully, they would be approved by Ms. Sawyer and Mark would like them. She called Mark to let him know she was now heading home and would call him when she got there.

He thought it would be best if he just waited for her at the apartment, rather than follow her around. She was being cautious and becoming more aware of her surrounding. He could tell, she was looking around more. He also noticed she was on her cell phone a lot more than usual. No doubt with her bed buddy. All sluts have bed buddies. He needed to be very careful when playing this out because her bed buddy was a cop. He really didn't care. He was going to take her tomorrow and have her for a while then he was going to kill her.

Jade got back to Mark's apartment and that old feeling came back. She new someone was following her. The feeling was really strong. She quickly retrieved the bags from her car, walked to the entrance of the building and took the elevator to Marks apartment. Once inside, she made sure the door was locked and she called Mark.

"I know someone is following me. I can't shake this feeling."

"Did you see anyone?" Mark asked.

"No, I didn't, and I looked around, but nothing. Its just this feeling."

"Stay there and make sure the door is locked. I'll be home soon. Don't worry about dinner. I'll bring home some Chinese food. Love you."

"Love you too honey."

It was almost six p.m. and Ross, and Shapiro were nearing the end of their day. Ross couldn't wait to get home to Jade. His phone began to ring. Looking at the caller ID, it was Dr. Lind. Ross looked at Shapiro and said, "here we go."

"What do you have Doc?"

"Milo Hamilton is not your killer. His DNA sample did not match the killers DNA. The test was repeated twice. However, there are genetic markers that match the killers, so Milo and the killer are probably related. Both of them have genetic markers that have multiple matches to Judge Hamilton. The results from the paternity test won't be in for couple of days. I put a rush on it."

"Thanks Doc. I will let Shapiro know."

Ross was still trying to process the information when he told Shapiro about it. Shapiro was just looking at him dumbfounded.

"So, let me get this straight. Milo Hamilton is not our killer." Shapiro said.

"That's right." Ross confirmed.

"But Milo's DNA and the killer's DNA have many genetic markers that match which suggests they are some how related."

"Your right again." Ross confirmed.

"And both Milo and the killer have many genetic markers that match Judge Hamilton's DNA sample." Shapiro said.

"Give the man a prize. Your right again."

"Ross, I don't need a god damn paternity test to tell me that Judge Hamilton has another son out there. That would explain why he had the fear of God look on his face when I made that remark about having two sons, the last time we were in his chambers."

"I was thinking the same thing. We just can't go barging in without proof. Lets wait till we get proof and throw it in his face." Ross said rationally.

"You know Ross, I think he won't want his lawyer present when we tell him what we know. I don't think his family knows he has another son out there."

"I guess we'll find out soon enough."

They both left the station for the day.

Jade was sitting on the couch, watching T.V., when she heard the door open, and she saw Mark coming in. She was so happy to see him. She got up and went to him and wrapped her arms around his neck and kissed him. He kissed her back. She took the Chinese food from him and placed it on the kitchen counter. She grabbed two plates from the cupboard above the sink, cutlery from the drawer under the counter, and napkins from the pantry, and set them on the placemats on the kitchen table. Mark meanwhile had gone to wash up and change into a pair of lounging paints and old tee shirt.

"How are you doing honey. Still scared?" Mark was concerned.

"Once I got home, I was fine. I locked the door and kept myself busy."

"I'm glad to hear that. You're going to keep doing the same thing you're doing now. When you're out, just let me know what you're doing and where you are. Always have your cell phone on you. Not in your purse, but on your body."

"Why?"

"Because you never know when you'll need it, sweetheart."

"I will Mark. No worries."

"Oh, I always worry about you honey."

They both sat down at the table and devoured the Chinese food. Jade hadn't eaten all day and Mark had a sandwich.

"Mark, I wanted to show you two colors I thought would be really nice for our place. There both in the gray family and are light."

"Jade, I already told you whatever you choose is fine with me. I don't know about colors. Just look around. That should tell you, I'm not an expert in interior design. Your place in the Sault was beautiful. I trust you honey. Our place will be beautiful."

"I'm happy that you trust me with decorating our home. But it's "our" home and I want you to be a part of it. I don't want you to just move in when its time. Do you want this or not? Are you excited about moving in with me because I can't wait to move in with you?"

"I'm sorry Jade. Of course, I'm excited about moving in with you. I love coming home to you. I just don't have the time right now to view the apartment, sign papers or decorate. If you want me to see the apartment, then I will but it will have to be on the weekend. Why don't we do that. Ask the superintendent if we can both see it this weekend."

"I know Mark. I know you don't. I just want you as excited as I am about moving in together."

"I am Jade, but you won't see me picking out colors or furniture. That's not me. I don't get overly excited about stuff like that, to be honest. As a cop, that's the way I've been trained. We have to keep our cool. Now if it was a seventy-inch TV, that's different." He smirked.

"Okay Mr. Cool, I get it."

They enjoyed a glass of wine, while watching T.V. and then went to bed.

CHAPTER 27

ROSS AND SHAPIRO WERE GOING over the written report Dr. Lind had completed for their files regarding the DNA samples for Milo Hamilton and Judge Hamilton. What they really wanted were the results regarding the paternity test.

"What happens if the paternity test is positive. Then what? We don't know about another son." Ross wondered.

"Then we apply pressure on the good old Judge. Like I said before, and I will say it again, the man is hiding something." Shapiro was adamant.

"Its hard to get your head around processing all this information." Ross admitted.

"It can be when you're processing other information, which has nothing to do with the case." Shapiro knew his partner's head was somewhere else.

"What are you talking about Shapiro?"

"You've had something on your mind since you came in. I can always tell. Is Jade, okay?"

"I'm worried about this feeling she has about someone following her. With this lunatic on the loose, I'm worried. I just feel that its too much of a coincidence that Jade's sister is murdered by a psychopath and now she feels that she's being followed. Maybe, I'm just being paranoid. I told her last night to keep her cell phone on her person, not her purse. She asked me why and I told her that you never know when you may need it."

"Mark, you're protecting her. You didn't want to scare her. If she carries the phone on her person, then we can ping the phone for her location, if she goes missing. I get it."

"I don't want to think that way, but as a cop, there's no other way I'm going to think. I want to keep her safe. Other than keeping her hostage in the apartment, I don't know what to do."

"You're doing it right now. You know where she is. She calls you when she leaves and calls when she arrives. You don't go out but rather, go home to her. Besides putting a tracker on her, I don't know what else you can do. You can't be with her 24/7. That's not realistic."

"I know, I know. I think right now I just need to focus on this case before I loose my mind. I will loose my mind if anything happens to her." Ross said.

"You really do love her."

"Yeah, I really do."

Jade wanted to get the paint swatches to Ms. Sawyer for approval. She wanted to do as much as she could while she had the time. Soon, her new job at the college would start. She has the next couple of weeks to pack her belongings and eventually move everything here. She would like to paint before bringing anything in to the apartment. She can't paint without approval. She let Mark know she was going over to the new apartment to bring Ms. Sawyer the paint swatches for approval.

Ross and Shapiro were heading out for lunch when Ross' phone started to ring. He checked the caller ID, and it was Dr. Lind.

"Dr. Lind what do you have for us?"

"I have the results of the paternity test and I can tell you Judge Hamilton and the killer are father and son. Detective Ross are you there?" Dr. Lind heard nothing.

Ross was stunned. "Yeah, I'm here! Just in shock, is all. Thanks Doc."

Shapiro was just staring at Ross. "So, what did he say!"

"He said that Judge Hamilton and our killer are father and son."

"Holy shit. Are you kidding me? I knew it. The Judge was and still is hiding something. We need to talk to him ASAP. Time to go back to the court house."

Jade was just leaving the new apartment. Ms. Sawyer told her the new colors would be no problem. The management team would approve them without a problem. Jade believed; Ms. Sawyer had quite a bit of influence on the team. She would still wait for the phone call to make sure. She was walking to her car when her cell phone began to ring.

"Hello"

"Hello Jade, its Rodney. Long time no talk. How are you doing?

"Hi Rodney. I'm good, how are you?"

"I'm well thank you. I was just wondering if you would meet me for a quick coffee. I have some of your sisters personal items. She must have left them at the hospital. I thought you would want them."

"Um, sure why not? Where would you like to meet."

"Well, we can meet at the hotel you were staying at. I know you don't know the city all that well. Meet me at the restaurant there in a half hour. Does that sound okay?"

"Sure, that sounds fine Rodney. See you then."

Jade got into the car and called Mark to let him know where she was going and at what time. She also let him know she was meeting Rodney Martins and why. He must be busy, she thought, because his phone went to voice mail. Jade left a message.

Ross and Shapiro were back at Judge Hamilton's chambers, talking with his assistant.

"Once again detectives, you don't have an appointment. The Judge is busy going over files in his chambers."

"Let him know that we are here, and we are not going anywhere. It is imperative we speak with him. Tell him if he wants to get his lawyer that's fine, but he should talk to us first."

The Judge came to the door, "detectives, I've told you before that I won't speak with you again without my lawyer. What can you possibly want now?"

"Judge Hamilton it would be in your best interest if you heard us out first and then made your choice as to whether you want to call your lawyer or not. I have a feeling that you won't want to make that phone call after you hear what we have to say." Shapiro told him.

"Fine then, come in. You have two minutes to tell me what you want to tell me, before I call my lawyer. I won't be manipulated by you two. Understand."

"First, your son Milo's DNA was not a match to the perp's DNA. Milo's been cleared." Ross said.

"How did you get his DNA? The Judge asked.

Ross explained how the DNA sample was obtained.

"I told you both you wouldn't find anything using his DNA." Judge Hamilton sounded relieved.

"You were right, we didn't find anything with his DNA, however his DNA and the killer's DNA have quite a few genetic markers that are a match. This suggests that they are probably related."

"That's crazy, how can they be related? You have one-minute left before I call my lawyer because I don't like what you are telling me."

"Wait it gets better, Judge Hamilton. We had a paternity test done on your DNA and the killer's and guess what we found out? We found out that you and the killer are related as well, more like father and son." Shapiro finally got to say what he wanted to say. He knew the judge was involved somehow.

The Judge went pale and began hyperventilating. Shapiro and Ross went to him and assisted him into his chair. He was profusely diaphoretic and was now short of breath. Shapiro and Ross thought he was having a heart attack. At best, he was having an anxiety attack.

"Judge Hamilton are you alright, do you need medical attention?"

Ross ran out to the reception area and told the assistant to get Judge Hamilton a cold glass of water. The young man brought one back in no time. Ross went back into the Judge's chambers.

"Judge Hamilton drink this. Take your time. Breath, just breath."

Ross and Shapiro waited with the Judge until he came around. He was still pale, but his breathing was better. The Judge undid the top three buttons of his shirt.

"This can't be happening, after all these years. It can't be. It just can't be." The Judge kept repeating himself.

"Judge Hamilton if there's something you need to tell us. Now would be a good time." Shapiro prompted.

"I was married before. A long time ago. I was twenty-five and thought I was in love. The young lady I was with became pregnant and I wanted to do the right thing, so I married her. Six months later, a son was born. He was healthy and beautiful. I was in my last year of law school in Toronto. As time went on, I realized I wasn't in love with Jean, and we became distant. We divorced a little over a year after we were married. Jean was so angry with me; she kept my son from me. I didn't really put up a fight. I was just starting my career. She remarried and moved away without telling me where she went. I moved to Sudbury several years later, opened my practice, married, and had a family. My wife and children don't know about my previous marriage and my son. I thought it best not to say anything. I thought about my son often. I wondered what he looked like, what he amounted to in life and hoped he had a good life. Now, your telling me this son, my son, is the man that killed Catherine. It can't be. You're wrong."

"Judge Hamilton, the paternity test is conclusive. I'm sorry." Ross explained.

Judge Hamilton put his face in his open palms and kept shaking his head. He was distraught.

"I can't believe a child of mine is a murderer. Why? What happened to this boy? What would cause him to kill another human being?"

"Judge Hamilton, Catherine is not the only person he has murdered. We know of one other women definitely, and possibly another woman in Toronto, years ago." Shapiro said.

"Oh my God. This just keeps getting worse. Those poor woman. Those poor parents, what they must have gone through and are still probably going through."

"So, you have had no contact with this son at all?" Shapiro asked.

"None. I tried to look for him several years later, but I couldn't locate him. I looked into the Board of Education of Toronto, thinking I could find the school he attended, but I think when Jean got married, she had my son's last name changed to her new husband's surname. Her family wouldn't tell me anything about their whereabouts. I was like the plague to them. I hired a private investigator, but he couldn't find anything except the name of her new husband. There was no internet or social media back then and finding someone or information about them, was more difficult."

"What was the name of her new husband?" Ross said.

"The private investigator found out it was John Martins."

"What? Say that again." Ross demanded.

"John Martins" The Judge repeated.

"What is your son's name, Judge Hamilton?" Ross asked.

"Jean and I named him Rodney after my father."

Both Shapiro and Ross looked at each other. Rodney Martins was his name, as in Dr. Rodney Martins.

"Are you telling me my son is a doctor? As a doctor, what reason would he have for doing this? He's supposed to heal people, not kill them. This can't be happening. Can't be happening."

Ross pulled out his phone to call Moore and Gladstone, explained why they needed to pick up Dr. Martins at the hospital and noted there was a message waiting for him. He had turned his phone off to question Judge Hamilton. It was Jade, telling him she was meeting Rodney Martins at the hotel restaurant as he had some personal belongings of her sister's, he found at the hospital and wanted to give them to her. Ross looked at his watch and noted the message was left almost forty-five minutes ago.

Shapiro noticed the panic in Ross' face and went to him. "What is it?

"Listen to this. Ross played the message back."

"Jesus Christ! We need to get to the restaurant."

They just ran out of the Judge's chambers, telling the assistant to keep an eye on the Judge. They sped all the way to the hotel.

"She always answers her phone. Pick up baby, pick up for Christ sakes." Ross was worried.

CHAPTER 28

Taking her was easier than he thought. She met him as planned and then he asked her to come to his car. He told her he put everything into a box for her and she could just pick it up and put it in her car. When she was close enough to his car, he used a cloth with chloroform, and she basically fell into his car. He drove her back to his stepfather's old house in Vermillion Lake.

The house was old. It was just a shell. No one had lived in it for years. The grass around it was overgrown and the shingles were falling off. The closest house was a half a mile away. After his stepfather died, he thought he would use it as his "playroom," rather than sell it. After all, it couldn't be traced back to him. His condo was in the city. He didn't' bring Jade downstairs to the "dungeon," rather he put her in one of the upstairs bedrooms and tied her wrists and ankles together. It was just a mattress on the floor. The windows were all covered and nailed shut. He knew she would be out for hours. He had also decided that after he killed Jade, he was leaving Sudbury. Three murders, its time to move on, he thought.

Ross and Shapiro got to the hotel and noticed Jade's car in the parking lot. Her purse was in the car. She wouldn't go anywhere without her purse. The car was locked so Ross couldn't tell if she had her phone on her. Ross tried calling Jade again, but there was no answer. He was scared.

He called Officer Tilley back at the station. "Tilley, I need you to find out everything you can on a Rodney Martins. He's a doctor at Holy Angels and drives a white Lexus. I need to know where he lives and anything else you can find. His stepfather's name is John Martins. See what you can find out about him as well. I need you to find it, like yesterday. When you find out about his car, put out a B.O.L.O. on it.

Ross notice Shapiro on the phone. "Thanks Gladstone, I'll tell him." "Martins isn't at the hospital. He apparently has taken several days off. He is not scheduled back till next week."

"Son of a bitch planned this all out. I know he has Jade. We need to find her Al. I can't lose her now. I just found her. We're planning a life together."

"We'll find her Mark, we'll find her. You're not sure if she has her phone but you told her to keep it on her right."

"Well lets ping her phone. Judge Hamilton will give us the warrant we need."

Shapiro called Judge Hamilton and explained what had happened. "Of course, I will sign a warrant to have this young lady's phone pinged. Anything to help. Consider it done."

Ross called Tilley back. "Tilley ask Levi to ping Jade Rose's cell phone. Ross rhymed off the phone number. Judge Hamilton is providing the warrant. If Levi doesn't feel comfortable about it, tell him to call Judge Hamilton. I need the location A.S.A.P."

"Will do Detective Ross. I'm on it"

Ross hung up his cell phone and noticed Shapiro was talking to the front desk clerk. Maybe someone saw something. Ross couldn't think right now. He was numb and just going through the motions. Thank God Shapiro was the rational one. Ross noticed Shapiro was writing something down in his black book. Ross was going into the hotel.

As Ross was walking in, Shapiro was walking out. Ross stopped and met him in the lobby. "The front desk clerk, Tracy, saw Jade leaving with a man that matches Martins description. Tracy recognized Jade right away. She also said they left in a black sedan with tinted windows about ten, fifteen minutes ago. Tracey explained, "it looked like she was helping this guy get something out of the back seat of his car. Then, he reached in, looked like he was trying to help her, and she just fell into the back seat of his car. It was odd."

"She fell into the car because she was drugged, that's why." Ross said, now really scared.

"Shapiro just got off the phone again with Judge Hamilton. I called the station and got Levi to track the GPS for any and all of Martins vehicles. So far, we know he has a black sedan and a white Lexus. We might as well use everything we can to find this asshole. The quicker we find him, the quicker we find Jade. Lets go back to the station. We can talk to Levi, Moore, and Gladstone there. Maybe, if we put our heads together, we can figure out where she is. Come on partner."

A couple of hours had passed. Ross was just sitting at his desk, staring at nothing. Shapiro was worried about his partner. "Mark we're going to find her. We are."

"Detectives," Officer Tilley said.

They both looked up at him. "Got something Tilley?" Ross said.

"Rodney Martins was born Rodney Hamilton to Jean and Theodore Hamilton in 1982. His parents divorced in 1983. Jean Hamilton married John Martins in 1985. Rodney was given his stepfather's surname. The family moved to Barrie, Ontario soon after the marriage to be closer to John's family in Sudbury. From what I can tell, Rodney had a decent upbringing. His stepfather was construction worker, and his mother was a homemaker. He was a straight "A" student. Attended the University of Toronto, Faculty of Medicine and completed medical school in 2007. He completed his residency in emergency medicine in Sudbury. He's been working at Holy Angels Hospital for the last ten years. He has a condo at Lakeview and of course you know about his vehicles. He has a clean record. Not even a parking ticket. I'm still working on John Martins."

"He must have known Jordan Lenski from medical school. She must have done something to piss him off. He knew Skylar from the hospital, and she must have done something to piss him off. Macy was the one that he didn't know, and probably was just a random kill. Macy's mouth would have pissed off anyone." Ross said.

Levi interrupted the conversation. "We're still waiting on the warrants for the GPS tracking and pinging the phone. The supervisor of the department won't allow it unless we have the warrants, signed and in hand. He's by the book."

"Does the supervisor know that someone's life is on the line? What the hell is his problem? What's taking so long? I called the Judge about an hour ago." Shapiro was irritated.

"The problem is that its late in the day. The warrants will get here soon. Moore and Gladstone are gone to check out his condo. They obtained the intern's address and are going to rattle his cage as well. He wasn't at the hospital when they were there earlier." Ross said.

Detectives Moore and Gladstone arrived at Rodney Martins' condo but there was no answer. Moore thought, expensive place, right on the water. The grounds keeper said he hadn't seen him for a couple of days and thinks he's gone away. He remembers Rodney saying he had a couple of days off at the hospital. The grounds keeper doesn't know of any other place in town or cottage that Rodney would go to.

"Judge Mallory wouldn't give us a warrant to search his residence. Said there wasn't enough probable cause. Judge Hamilton needed to go to the hospital. He was having trouble breathing, So we're out of luck right now." Moore said.

From Paris Street, they couldn't see any lights on in Martins condo. He wasn't there. They were going to see the intern next.

Moore and Gladstone arrived at small house in the Flour Mill District. The intern, Morgan Sinclair was renting a basement apartment. The detectives went round back and knocked on the door. "Mr. Sinclair; Detectives Moore, and Gladstone. We need to speak to you. Open the door please."

Morgan Sinclair came to the door with a towel wrapped around his waist. "What is this? What do you want?"

Gladstone got right down to business. "Have you seen Dr. Rodney Martins?"

"No"

"When was the last time you saw him." Gladstone asked.

"I don't know." Sinclair was cocky.

"Listen to me you cocky son of a bitch, we have a missing woman, and we believe the good doctor has abducted her, so think really hard when I ask you questions. When was the last time you saw him?"

Sinclair could see Gladstone was serious and wasn't going to put up with his bullshit. "We were at the hospital finishing a night rotation three mornings ago. That was the last time I saw him. He said he was going away for a couple of days. Dr. May has taken over my residency, in his absence."

"Did he say anything about where he was going?"

"No, nothing. He wasn't really the talkative kind. It was all about medicine and what a brilliant doctor he was. The man is full of himself. That's my opinion."

From inside the apartment, a female voice was heard, "hey Morgan, you coming back to bed?"

Gladstone made it very clear to Sinclair that if Martins contacts him, he is to contact the police. "You understand me?"

"Yeah, I understand." Sinclair shut the door and went back to whatever he was doing.

"It appears, we interrupted his plans for the evening. Oh well, that's too bad." Moore said sarcastically.

Jade was still out cold. "I must have put more chloroform on the cloth than I should have, he thought." He thought Jade was different. He wanted to talk to her and explain why he did what he did before he killed her. "See, I can be compassionate when I want to be." He laughed. He hated her. He was going to enjoy hearing her scream when he hurt her. He wanted to see the fear in her eyes after the bullshit she had put him through.

Shapiro was worried about his partner. Ross had hardly spoken. He wanted to go out there and pound the pavement looking for her, but it would be best if he stayed here and worked on angles from the station. He was a loose canon right now. If he had found Martins, he would kill him first and ask questions later. "What do we have Al, anything new."

"We know Martins hasn't been home for a couple of days and the last time his intern saw him was three mornings ago. We checked; he doesn't have any other properties he could go to. Nothing in his name. We're still checking on the stepfather. We also know his mother and stepfather died shortly after he started his position at Holy Angels Hospital. They died a short time apart from each other. Death certificates indicate they died of normal circumstances, but you never know. He's a doctor."

Pino Levi, the computer specialist came downstairs and was walking straight to Shapiros' desk. All heads turned.

"Give me good news Levi. We got the warrants for GPS tracking and pinging of the cell phone. Unfortunately, we couldn't get a GPS location on the cars. He must have turned off the GPS tracking. As far as the phone, we are having trouble with the signal. This could be due to the remoteness of the location or the location period. Maybe, the location has no cell towers. Sometimes the person needs to move a few feet for a clear signal. Unfortunately, we need a little more time. I know time is not on our side, but that's the best I can do right now."

"Thanks Levi. Keep at it and let us know the second you got anything."

Ross was pacing now. "Al all we have now is Jade's cell phone. Otherwise, we have nothing. She must have the phone on her. If it were still in her purse, the location would have been picked up without a problem, at the hotel. Why is it taking so long to find out about whether his stepfather had property here or not?"

"Mark, only in the movies do they solve a crime in an hour. In the real world it takes time. I know you don't want to hear that right now, but you need to keep your head on straight or you won't be any good to anyone. We're all here doing what we have to do. None of us are going home tonight."

CHAPTER 29

JADE WAS STARTING TO COME around. She was having a tough time focussing. She couldn't keep her eyes open or her head up. Her mouth was so dry, it felt like sand. Where was she? What happened to her?

"There you are Jade. Nice to see you getting up finally. I was getting worried about you. I thought perhaps, I used a lethal amount of chloroform." Martins said.

Jade was still trying to focus and was going in an out of grogginess. She didn't recognize the voice, although it was familiar. Her brain was to foggy. She couldn't process it."

"Come on Jade get up. Its time to get up. We need to talk, you and I."

Jade was starting to open her eyes. She was blinking a lot. She finally opened her eyes and could process the face and voice. Oh my God, it was Rodney Martins. "Its you." Jade was speechless.

"Yes, its me. Finally, I have been dreaming of this day since you abruptly left our dinner date."

Jade was scared. He could see the fear in her face and body language. She kept moving around until she finally sat up and placed her arms around her knees which she had brought close to her body. This also kept her steady, as she was still slightly groggy. She noticed her wrists and ankles were bound together with rope. "What have you been dreaming of Rodney?"

"I've been dreaming of you and I together since I met you but then you blew me off for your detective friend. That wasn't nice. Your sister did the same thing and she paid for it dearly."

"My sister! What are you talking about? You said you hardly knew my sister. Are you saying, you killed my sister?"

"Yes, I did. Your sister was leading me on. She would go out with me then the intern came along, and she blew me off. Then she would see me again and blow me off again. She would have sex with him but not with me. She was nothing but a slut, just like you. You're both tramps. You're parents would be so proud of the sluts they raised." He laughed.

Jade couldn't believe what he was saying. He was insane. The look in his eyes was that of a madman, not a healing doctor. She needed to keep him talking. She needed to buy herself more time.

"Rodney men and women go out with each other and sometimes things just don't work out. So, they move on and eventually, hopefully they meet the one they want to spend the rest of their lives with. Their objective is not to hurt or reject anyone. Its about finding the right person for you. If I hurt you or you felt rejected, that was never my intention and I'm sorry."

He came right up to her and grabbed her chin hard. "No that's how sluts and tramps interact. A lady wouldn't do that. I don't want your apology." He let go of her chin and went back to where he was sitting before.

I better just shut up and listen to him, she thought. Obviously, he didn't want to hear anything she had to say. She couldn't believe he killed Skylar. She needed to get out of here.

"When I was a baby, my father left my mother and me. My mother would say he just didn't love us enough to stay. My mother got married to another man, who was a good provider but not a good husband or father. I spent a lot of time with my mother. All my mother kept saying is that my father rejected me, he rejected me. She blamed me for my father leaving. I found out years later that it was her that he didn't love and that my father had attempted to find me, but my mother's family refused to tell him, where I was. Eventually, he just gave up. I worked hard and put myself through medical school. I wanted to find him and show him what I had become. I found him in Sudbury, that's why I took the job at Holy Angels Hospital. I found out he was a Judge. I drove by his house one day and saw him with what I presumed was his wife, children, and grandchildren. They were all smiling and carrying on. I was infuriated. His life went on and he was happy, while my life was empty of love and happiness. He had a new family. He didn't need me anymore."

Jade just stared at him. He was in a daze. All he was doing now was breathing heavy. It seemed like he had gone to another place, and he was furious. "Where are you, Mark? Where are you?" She kept asking herself.

Levi came flying down the stairs, "we got a hit. Her phone is pinging somewhere in Vermillion Lake. The exact location is still giving us a problem, but we're working on it."

Ross and Shapiro looked at each other and grabbed their jackets. "We're going there now. Its about a thirty-five, forty-minute ride. Call us if there is anything new. At least we'll be closer than we are now. Gladstone and Moore, can you cross check any properties owned out there with the last name Martins?"

"Sure, you got it." Moore said.

Dr. Martins came out of his daze a few minutes later, like nothing ever happened. "I was in love once, while I was in medical school, I thought she was in love with me too, but I was wrong. In our last year of medical school before our residency she told me she didn't love me and needed to explore what was out there. She said that I lacked emotional intimacy and she needed more from a man. She said that my mother scared her, and she blamed everyone else for her problems but herself. Her name was Jordan Lenski, and she was right about my mother. My mother was troubled. I think that was the problem between her and my father. Nevertheless, I was very hurt and felt rejected by her. I followed Jordan one night and saw her with one of the University's hockey jocks. They were in one of the change rooms, after everyone left and they were going at it like rabbits. He had his mouth and hands everywhere. It was obvious, she enjoyed being with him. I could hear her calling out his name while coming unraveled. I met up with her later and talked her into being with me one last time, for old times' sake. For three days I gave her what she wanted, and she was in her glory. Of course, I got what I wanted as well. The only thing is that I didn't want her anymore. She was just a slut. I wanted a woman who would love me. Not someone who would give herself to anybody and everybody. I made sure she knew, before I killed her, that I could give her what she wanted, but she chose to throw me away."

He was insane. That look was back in his eyes. Jade needed to know why he killed her sister. If she was going to die, she needed to know. "Rodney why did you kill my sister?"

"Your sister was the biggest slut of all. She kept leading me on. Flirting with me but wouldn't go out with me. One night I followed her from her apartment to her friend Kim's place. She went in looking like Skylar and came out looking like a barbie doll. Blonde wig, lots of make up and tight-fitting dresses. She looked like a tramp. She got into a cab, and I followed her to the Windsor Park Hotel. I knew what she was doing there. I just didn't know who she was doing it with, so I decided to go inside and put myself in a little corner. When I saw who was escorting her off the elevator, all I felt was rage. I wanted to kill them both. It was my father, the Honourable Judge Theodore Hamilton. He was having an enjoyable time with your sister. His wife wasn't enough, I guess. Your sister didn't want to be with me, but she would have sex with an old man for money. She rejected me but had no problem being with my father.

"Your father." Jade was stunned.

"Yes, the judge was my father. Your sister didn't know, but I didn't care. Anyway, I went over to her apartment one night. I stopped by on the premise that I had a book for her that she wanted. I saw Morgan Sinclair's car in the visitor's parking. As you know, her apartment was on the bottom floor at the back of the building, so no one saw me going around. She had lace drapes and a night light on in her bedroom, so I could see them. They were enjoying each other in every way possible for a couple of hours. I enjoyed watching them. Your sister gave as good as she got. A short time after Morgan left, I called her from the parking lot, telling her I had her book and asked her to come out and get it. She did and when she turned her back, I took her. It was so easy. Just like you. I enjoyed the fear in her eyes before I killed her."

Jade thought of her little sister. She wanted to kill this monster with her own bare hands. He couldn't deal with rejection, so he chose to eliminate the problem. As much as she wanted to tell him he was crazy and she hated him, and not worthy of her sister, she needed to play it cool, or he would kill her. She still needed more time.

Ross' phone was ringing. It was Levi. Ross, we have and address for you. The house is on Vermillion Lake Road. We crossed checked it with the Martins name and it was passed on to John Martins but was still under his father's name, Alfred Martins. That's why it was hard to find. The phone is still pinging from around there. This has to be the place." Levi rambled off the address.

Ross told Shapiro everything and they started driving. They weren't far. "Its dark out here, we could miss the house. My wife lived out here when we were dating. I know my way around. We're going to turn off the car lights just before the driveway and park the car, so he doesn't know we're coming." Shapiro said.

"Sounds good to me." Ross just wanted Jade safe and would do anything for her, even if that meant die for her."

Jade had to keep him talking. "What about the young prostitute that was murdered? I heard about it on the news.

"Oh yes, the whore Macy. She was a spitfire. Had a comeback for everything. Her mouth got her into trouble even though at times it was very useful, if you know what I mean. I went looking for release and met up with Macy. My intention was never to kill her but just to have fun with her. Her mouth was worse than a trucker's mouth. That girl knew how to have fun. She orgasmed over and over for me. All I had to do was touch her. I found her under the Bridge of Nations. Her friend had left early in the morning, but Macy was still out. After our encounter, she told me that she would never want me again for any amount of money, because I called her a slut. She rejected me for calling a spade a spade. I took her when she was walking back from our encounter, and I brought her back here. She called the room downstairs "the dungeon."

Jade didn't want to hear anymore. She knew he was being graphic on purpose. "The asshole," she thought. He was disgusting. He didn't know how to truly love a woman. He couldn't feel love. He was truly a narcissist and a psychopath. It was all about him and how he felt.

Ross and Shapiro were now around the house. They could hear talking but couldn't see anything. The windows were all covered. The house had no electricity going to it, so the light they saw must be from a kerosene or propane lamp. They called for back up and continued to survey the house. Shapiro was round back and saw a white Lexus and black Audi sedan parked there. He moved to the front and whispered to Ross, "he's here. Both cars are in the back." They knew they had to find a way in but had to remain quiet and use the element of surprise to their advantage.

Jade could see that crazed look in his eyes. He was rubbing himself on the outside of his pants. Jade could see, he was getting hard.

"Now, Jade its your turn. You lied to me the evening we had gone out for dinner. You said that you were full of emotion because you had gone over to your sister's apartment for the first time since she was killed, and you just wouldn't be good company. I saw Detective Ross coming into the hotel as I was leaving, after I dropped you off. He didn't see me. I came back to your room and could hear both of you talking, more like you yelling at him. I know you didn't plan on him showing up. I could tell by what you were saying to him. I thought because you were angry at him, you were going to kick him out of the hotel room. But you didn't. I waited for him to leave but his car was still there in the morning. I guess you weren't to full of emotion to have sex him. Were you Jade? Did your eyes roll back in your head? Well, Jade I'm going to make you scream. He was now coming towards her. He had a knife in his hands."

"Jade started screaming at him, telling him to stay away from her."

He approached her, "you can scream all you want Jade. No one will hear you out her." He was moving closer. When he got close enough, she pushed him back by raising her legs. He didn't fall back very far, but he did fall. She caught him off guard.

"Your going to pay for that, you bitch." He was angry.

As he was getting up, the front door was kicked open and Ross ran towards the bedroom where he heard her screaming. He was calling out her name, with his gun leading the way. Shapiro had kicked in the back door at the same time, and he had his gun ready. Rodney was getting up quickly and grabbed the knife he had dropped. He was going towards Jade with it. Ross entered the room and saw Rodney rushing towards Jade with the knife lifted above his head, ready to stab her. Ross shot Rodney twice in the chest. He dropped to the floor. Shapiro entered the room and removed the knife away from the area. He checked Martins for a pulse but couldn't find one. Rodney Martins was dead. Shapiro waited outside for back up that was on the way.

Ross was down on both knees, with his arms around Jade. Are you alright? Talk to me." Ross demanded.

Jade was crying, "I knew you would come for me. I put my phone in my jacket pocket. I knew you would come for me."

Ross looked at her with both his hands holding her face, "I would die for you Jade. I love you. I was so scared I was going to loose you."

"He killed Skylar, he killed Skylar. He killed them all. He's insane. He drugged me and was going to kill me too."

"I know Jade, I know honey. We got him. He won't hurt anyone anymore."

"Get me out of this hell, Mark. Get me out of here and take me home."

"First you go to the hospital to be checked out, then I'll take you back home with me. Let the doctors check you out. With me there of course."

EPILOGUE

Six months later

THE MURDER CASES OF SKYLAR Rose, Macy Collins and Jordan Lenski were officially closed. There was overwhelming evidence in the basement of the Vermillion Lake home. Dr. Rodney Martins was a serial killer. There was blood evidence, hair, fibers, and the murder weapon with his fingerprints on it. With regards to the murder of Jordan Lenski, Jade told Detective Hill from Toronto Police Services what Rodney had confessed to her before he tried to kill her. Rodney Martins was questioned years ago but he had created a solid alibi for himself, just like he did with Skylar.

After the ordeal, Jade was released from hospital. Mark had taken some time off of work to be with her and make sure she was physically fine. While off, they utilized that time to move her belongings to Sudbury, paint the apartment, purchase furniture, and decorate.

Physically Jade was fine, but emotionally, at times, she still had nightmares. At first, they were bad, but now she is having them less and less. Jade refused medication to help her sleep. She continues to cry over her sister and what Skylar probably went through the last days of her life, at the hands of Dr. Rodney Martins. He had everybody fooled. He came across as being so helpful, kind and caring but he was totally the opposite. He only cared about himself. He was evil.

Jade loved her new job at the college. Her and Cam had become very close friends and were planning a girls weekend in Toronto, for much-needed shopping and pampering. Jade was looking forward to it.

Judge Hamilton's name was kept out of the media. Afterall, he didn't have anything to do with the murders. He did retire as his health was not the best. Emotionally, he had difficulty living with what a child of his had done. Its not known if he told his wife and family about Rodney. The police suspect that Rodney Hamilton a.k.a. Rodney Martins not only killed three woman, but also his mother and stepfather.

Both Shapiro and Ross knew Martins would have kept killing if he wasn't stopped. They believed he would have moved from Sudbury and started killing elsewhere.

"Al come here; I want to show you something." Ross asked

Shapiro was looking at a beautiful solitaire diamond engagement ring. "You're going to ask her to marry you? Finally!"

"Its like you said, I knew I loved her after our first date. Yeah, I'm going to ask her tonight during dinner or maybe after dinner. I don't know. All I know is that I'm going to ask her. One more thing."

"What's that?"

"Will you be my best man. There's no one else I want. Your my best friend, you've been like a father to me, so what do you say?"

"Correction, I'm your only friend and don't forget it. Who else is going to put up with your crap." They both laughed. "Of course, I would be honoured to be your best man. You better ask her to marry you first and make sure she says yes, or you won't need a best man."

Mark was home for supper around six p.m. He and Jade had moved into there new place about five months ago. She painted and decorated. The apartment looked like a palace. The light colors made it refreshing to come home to. The kitchen was white and gray, the living room was a combination of blues and grays with an interesting area rug, in blues, yellows, grays and a touch of black. The navy-blue leather sectional had a matching ottoman. The faux black fireplace made it feel warm. Skylar's urn sat on top of the mantle. The guest bedroom was gray with some yellow tones and the master bedroom was whimsical blues, light grays, with lace curtains. It had a comfortable king bed in it. The bedrooms had silver-colored fans and plants as well. There were plants in the living room and pictures of family and friends and of course them.

"Hi honey, I didn't hear you come in."

"Hey babe. Dinner smells wonderful as per usual."

"Well, its ready so if you want to wash up, I'll dish it out."

"I'll be right back."

Mark took the box with the ring in it, out of his pocket and put it on top of his night stand. He would be back for it. He decided he would ask her after supper, while they're having their nightly glass of wine.

They ate in the dining room with views of the water. The view was incredible. "If someone had told me a year ago that I would be having a great supper, with the woman I love, in a home with water views, I would have told them they were out of their minds." Ross said.

"I know, I was thinking the same thing. I thank God everyday for what I have. You, our home, our relationship, our jobs. We're very fortunate."

"You're absolutely right babe. We are fortunate."

They had finished dinner and as usual it was terrific. They had moved to the living room with their glass of wine.

"Mark are you alright. You look pensive. What's on your mind/"

"Hold on a minute Jade, I'll be right back."

Mark walked back to the bedroom to retrieve the ring. He opened the box, looked at the ring and closed the box. He took a deep breath and walked back to the living room. He sat down beside Jade and took her hands in his.

"Jade, you know that I love you very much. I would do anything for you."

"I know that. I love you too very much. What's going on Mark?"

Mark brought the box out and Jade saw it. She looked at him and brough her hands to her face. She was full of emotion and had tears in her eyes. "Oh my God, Mark."

"Jade, will you marry me? Be my wife."

"Yes! Yes, I'll marry you!" She didn't have to think about it.

Mark placed the ring on the third finger of her left hand and then he kissed her. "I love you, Jade Rose."

AUTHOR BIOGRAPHY

Rudy Ann Putton is a registered nurse who has worked in various health care settings as a clinical nurse, nurse manager and educator. She knew she wanted to be a nurse at a young age.

Caring for people and helping them to heal allowed her to show the nurturing side of her personality but it was writing that allowed her to express her creative side. She began writing in college where she let her imagination run wild. She has always enjoyed writing romantic suspense. She calls this genre the best of both worlds. Writing became part of who she is.

Rudy Ann lives in Northern Ontario with her husband. She enjoys travelling, spending time with family and friends and a great cup of coffee or two…. or three.

.